G. Keller

Roach Girl origin trilogy two

G. Keller

Mileyjackmedia

Orlando, Florida

G. Keller

Roach Girl origin trilogy two

Mileyjackmedia, LLC

Orlando, Florida

This story was printed in the United States of America.

ISBN 979-8-9994287-1-4

The story, all names, characters, and incidents portrayed in this production are fictitious. No identification with actual persons (living or deceased), places, buildings, and products is intended or should be inferred.

Cover Art by Janelle Bell-Martin

This book is dedicated to my mom, who always told me not to get caught up in material possessions. She said, "They are just things."

G. Keller

"Materialism is like a gold chain around your neck. It's shimmery and shiny, but it's still a chain."

Dakotah A. Nawlins

G. Keller

Chapter One

Vivian

The Portofino Magazine was just a high class, glossy publication of advertisements pretending to be local news, except for the article about us. *Our* story was newsworthy. *Our* story made the cover of the magazine, and a six-page spread inside. *Our story* was not an advertisement but was bound to be good for RG Construction. Real Good Construction...aka (to me only) Roach Girl Construction. Our motto: *We are indestructible.*

I stared at all of us--dad, Mr. Cooper, Leo, Dexter, Freddy, Jamie, Cleo, Dushon and me--on the cover standing in front of our old home in Royal Palm Estates, with me holding the first-place ribbon. Our smiles were so wide someone might get swallowed up if the magazine came to life. I remember when we took the picture, we were all laughing hysterically because Dexter and Dushon kept dancing between the clicks of the photographer. The photographer loved it because she said the fun made great photos. She was right. This was a great photo. And the story about us inside was even better. Two teachers and their students from Lorenzo Williams Technical High School complete a unique and beautiful remodel in one of the premier gated communities of North Portofino, Florida, winning the top prize in the yearly construction remodeling contest put on by the Cambier County Home Builders Association.

I laid on my bed in my new room in our new home, a cozy beach-style cottage we just finished renovating. It was not the grand North Portofino estate we sold at a top price. In fact, the entire house was about the size of the kitchen and dining room of our old house, but I loved my small, new home with all my heart. I loved the pale blue paint we chose for the exterior and interior. The colors made me feel like I was living in a cool swimming pool every minute. I loved the white picket fence. I loved the white trim and window boxes. I loved the enormous yard with the giant banyan tree in front and the mango, lime, and orange trees in the back.

Today, dad and I were going to put flowers in the window boxes and work in the yard. He told me to get up early so we could beat the heat. Dad, too, loved this house with all his heart. When he wasn't teaching, he was working on our house, our yard, or the homes down the block we were renovating to sell. My dad was the happiest I had seen him in so long, and he hadn't touched a drop of alcohol in months. Gone was the stick figure emaciated body from last Christmas. Gone was the overgrown matted beard. Gone was the bleary, glassy-eyed stare and constant faint smell of wine.

I had my dad back. The sober dad. The functional dad. The happy dad.

But as I stared at this magazine cover and looked at all the happy faces, one nagging question would not leave me alone. It trickled up my spine in the middle of the night. It crawled up my arm when I tried to work. It penetrated and burrowed into every tiny crack in my Roach Girl brain.....where in the world was mom?

Victoria

"Victoria, what are you looking at?" Conrad's cellphone rang, interrupting his interrogation, and he abruptly got up to take the call, walking towards the cockpit.

I jumped up and opened the overhead compartment, sliding the magazine into a hard-to-find zippered pouch inside my suitcase. I would read the article later when he slept. I couldn't believe what I had just seen. Vivian, Collier and several other people on the cover of the Portofino Magazine, smiling happy smiles. Successful smiles. 'Look everyone, I made it' smiles.

Smiles that didn't include me.

But what did I expect? Isn't this what I wanted? I wrote it in the letter to Vivian. I left so that Collier would restart his life. And by the looks of him and Vivian laughing on the cover, he did. They were happy. Without me.

Maybe it was me all along who kept him from succeeding? I always blamed him for what went wrong. His drinking. His drunken accident leaving that man blind, getting sued, losing his medical license, leaving us broke, stopping our remodeling project, the one I was obsessed with. But looking at them so happy and successful without me there makes me think it was me causing Collier's problems. Was I too demanding? Too materialistic? Too judgy? Too pushy? Too bitchy? Yes. Yes. Yes, to all of it. But it is too late now. I made my choice. I left. And now I'm trapped in a world I can't escape. A world I deserved.

Chapter Two

Vivian

"Beautiful choice, Vivian," Dad and I stood back and admired the yellow and orange coreopsis flowers.

"I love window boxes," I sighed and pulled off my gardening gloves, wiping the sweat from my face with my t-shirt sleeve.

"The colors you picked go so well against the blue house. It looks like a million little sunshines against a clear blue sky," dad added.

I looked at dad smiling at the pretty flowers and house with such pride and peace on his face. I couldn't help but wish mom was here to see him like this. See how whole he was again, like in the old days when I was a little girl. When we were all a happy family. As mad as I was at her for walking out on me—on us, and how part of me never wanted to lay eyes on her again for what she put me through, another part of me wanted her to be standing right here with us, admiring the yellow and orange flowers.

Dad met my eyes and as soon as he saw the emotions pool up, his face softened to a knowing, compassionate look, and the dam broke with giant streams of tears cascading down my cheeks.

He pulled me close, and I didn't care if he was sticky with sweat. I let loose. "Why did she leave us, dad? Why? I love being here with you. You know I do. But it's just not the same without her. I hate her for leaving us. I hate her for breaking our family. I hate her," I said strongly through my clogged throat.

Dad gently pulled away from me and grabbed my shoulders with a loving firmness, like I had dreamt he would do all those months I was alone after mom and dad had deserted me. "Listen to me. Your mom did not break our family. I broke our family. Your mom is not the cruel person you think she is. She loves you. She was desperate and living with a severe addict. I am the only one to blame here. She tried to get me help so many times. She did not give up easily. I wore her out. Do not blame her for leaving. Blame me."

I looked at his face and saw it. I saw just how much he still loved her. After leaving us over a year ago with only a short letter to me saying goodbye and that she couldn't take it anymore and that she hoped her leaving would force dad to restart his life, he still loved her. *How?* How could he still love her after her departure almost killed him and left me abandoned? Anything could have happened in those months I was left alone. I could have been robbed, raped, killed or sent to foster care. Dad may have died in the Everglades had I not found him last Christmas. All of that would never have happened if mom hadn't left us. And yet, his face ached for her. I saw it. He still loved her despite everything that happened. All those months I spent alone after they left, I thought my parents' love for each other was over, dead. But looking at dad's face as he took the blame for her leaving, I could tell love was still there, from dad at least.

I wanted to be able to forgive her like he could. To love her like he did. To understand her like he was able to do. But I just couldn't do it. My mind was like a referee in a wrestling match between love and hate for her and hate always seemed to be winning.

He now had tears in his eyes, and I clung to him again. "I can't understand why she hasn't come back. To check on me. On us. How she disappeared like she did with no way of contacting her is what is so hurtful. I just need to know where she is in order to feel...... whole."

Dad and I just stood there holding each other. I opened my eyes and released my hug but kept one arm around his waist and gazed back at the window boxes, resting my head against his shoulder, leaning into him and thinking, *I wish she could see the window boxes with tiny sunshines. I wish she would come back and stay. I know the house isn't in a fancy neighborhood. I know the house isn't a mansion. I know the house isn't as grand as the homes in the remodeling magazines. But it had us. Why couldn't us be enough?*

Victoria

"Shut that damn window shade. The light is blinding me," Conrad barked. I quickly closed the shade tight so not a crack of light leaked out of the box-shaped window. We were flying above the clouds, and the brightness had filled the cabin of the plane. Now, it was a dark dungeon.

He shut his eyes and said, "Don't make a sound, so I can get a 30-minute rest before we land."

I wanted desperately to reach up to the overhead compartment and find the magazine. I wanted to read about Vivian and Collier and see pictures of the inside of our house. I had wanted that remodel so badly and waited so long, but it never happened. I gave up and left before I could see it completed. Now, I wanted to see how they finished it without me in the worst way. But I would have to wait. I couldn't risk disturbing Conrad.

I stared at his face that once seemed handsome and now repulsed me. I wanted to get as far away from him as possible. I looked over at the small, square window with its shade shut tight. It looked like a tiny box you could open, a window box. I imagined myself shrinking in size like Alice in Wonderland, opening it and jumping into the sky, cascading down through clouds and air, falling, falling, falling. I couldn't take my eyes off the window box. The exit that gave me a fantasy of freedom from my horrible reality.

Chapter Three

Vivian

"I need to get ready to go to Sharon's," We both started walking towards the garage to put away the gardening tools. "She wants me to help her organize new inventory this afternoon."

"I'm going to grab a sandwich and head over to the job site to meet the guys. We are working all afternoon," Dad said chugging a Gatorade.

"Don't forget, the Lamonts tonight," I reminded him.

I showered and changed into a pretty, pale blue designer dress I snatched from a lady who dropped off two large boxes of clothes last Saturday. She twirled her eyes when she set the boxes down and said her daughter *had* to have these clothes and then left for college saying she didn't want them anymore. I loved being the first one to see what comes into Sharon's Riches. I no longer worked in the back room away from customers. I was so good at putting combinations of clothing together that Sharon thought my talents were wasted hidden from view, but I always liked to check out the inventory before putting it on display. She also loved the teen corner I created, and my presence helped her sell this side of her high-end secondhand clothing shop.

Since summer began, I helped dad with the renovating three days a week and worked at Sharon's three days a week. I convinced Sharon to give a portion of the proceeds we made in the teen corner to the local homeless shelter. It didn't take too much convincing because ever since we found dad living in the Everglades, Mr. Cooper, Sharon, Dad and I decided to make the Portofino Homeless Shelter our charity of choice. When we sell the homes we are working on, we are giving part of the sale to the shelter.

"I love that dress on you. I knew the minute I saw it, it was meant for you," Sharon greeted me with a smile as I walked through the front door. "I have a ton of new clothes to organize. The spring cleaners have been busy. So many of the clothes coming in hardly look worn. I'm so excited."

I followed her to the back and got to work.

"Remember, when you hear the door ring, come out and help me. I want to show you off to my customers. You help me sell, sell, sell."

Sharon doted on me like a parent. However, no one would think Sharon was my mom, unless they

19

thought I was adopted. We looked the polar opposite of each other. Sharon's long, silky black hair, pale skin and big dark brown (almost black) eyes were a sharp contrast to my long, thick, wavy, wild blonde hair and light brownish-gold eyes, and my skin took naturally to the sun, giving me a constant pinky brown glow.

The door jingled, followed by a burst of laughter.

I walked straight out to the front of the store to help Sharon like I promised and froze. Falling all over each other laughing were Bella, Brianna, and Sarah. When they saw me, they froze, too.

"Hello," I tried my best to appear calm, while my heart went wild with rapid beating and my face went hot.

I heard Brianna whisper, "It's Roach Girl," and they all giggled.

I could tell by Sharon's hard look that she recognized Brianna from the time she came in with her mom and wanted one of my designer dresses. I could tell she was ready to rescue me if I needed her to—that parental instinct she now had for me. But I wasn't the same girl that hid in the back corner. I was proud of what Roach Girl turned me into. They could call me that all day long. I didn't care. To me Roach Girl meant strength. Resilience. Perseverance. Indestructibility. Roach Girl was badass.

I felt myself stand taller and suddenly, a calmness swept over me.

"Hi guys," I said cheerfully, not wanting them to think I cared whether they were there or not. "We have some really cute new items over here." I took charge, and they followed me.

I knew that many of the items would be too expensive for them, even though they were used items. Sharon only took top designer clothes, shoes, and handbags that looked new, and while they were technically secondhand and less money than new items would be, they still cost more than what Brianna and her gang could afford.

"We have some nice things on the clearance rack," I pointed where to look.

Brianna acted insulted and arrogantly said, "Show me the most unique and expensive stuff."

Startled, I turned and showed her some beautiful dresses.

Dramatically, she began looking and settled for a white Greek style halter dress and held it up to herself.

"That will look amazing on you," Sarah encouraged.

"Yes, try it on," added Bella.

21

Brianna went into the dressing room and came out with a twirl, "Don't you think Langston will looove this on me."

I knew she added that barb about Langston to try and make me jealous. I had absolutely no feelings for him anymore. Actually, I cringe when I think we were a couple for so long. He was a rude, social climbing, wanna-be elitist just like Brianna. They were meant for each other. Besides, I was in love with Leo, the most incredible, authentic boy I had ever known.

I wondered if she had seen the price tag. That dress was $450.

"I'll take it," Brianna announced and a few minutes later emerged from the dressing room.

I took the dress from her and said, "The dress is $450." As soon as I said it, I knew my tone sounded like I thought she couldn't afford it.

Her eyes narrowed, and she looked straight at me. "I know. I would like to look at shoes to go with it."

She found some gold strappy sandals and earrings bringing her total to $650.

Sarah found a handbag she wanted for $375, and Bella found a gold bracelet for $575.

Sharon went to the back to wrap everything up, and I led everyone to the cash register. Brianna pulled out the biggest wad of cash and started counting out one hundred-dollar bills. When she got to $700, she stopped, but she had a stack more that she shoved back into her bag.

Sarah and Bella both pulled out wads of cash, too. Did they just hit the lottery? Brianna, Bella, and Sarah weren't poor, but they all lived in Hidden Oaks, a middle-class neighborhood—as mom would say-- with cookie cutter houses, and I knew they didn't have tons of extra cash. Brianna's mom was a teacher, and her dad was a fireman. Bella's mom didn't work, and her dad was the manager at Home Depot, and Sarah's parents owned a small ice cream shop. I knew they didn't have wads of extra cash to give them for expensive clothes. This was strange.

While we waited for Sharon, Brianna sniffly asked, "How do you like Lorenzo?"

"I love it," I said, and I meant it. Going to the tech school instead of Gulfside High was the best decision I ever made. It led me out of a situation that seemed impossible. It led me away from Langston, Brianna, Bella, and Sarah. It led me to Leo. It led me to Dad. It led Dad to recovery and success. LWTHS was my savior.

"Do you guys have jobs now?" I asked them, wondering how they had so much cash.

They all giggled but said nothing.

Sharon burst from the back room with beautiful white boxes wrapped in gold bows.

They left, laughing at some secret joke, letting me know I wasn't part of their group anymore.

Little did they know what a relief that was.

Victoria

In the beginning, he was so charming, so persuasive, so attentive. In the beginning, I was vulnerable, thirsty for love, hungry for comfort, easy prey. In the beginning, I missed all the signs……..

"Welcome to McCormick's, can I help you find something?" I smiled.

"Whoever hired you needs a raise," he smiled back.

I took the bait and returned the flirtation, coyly. "Well, I do make the most sales in this joint."

"I bet you could sell a fur coat to the president of PETA and then have him eating steak out of your hand," the elegant and handsome older man continued. "Allow me to introduce myself. I'm Conrad McCormick, and I can see why this is my top producing store in the entire chain." He reached for my hand and kissed it innocently

with a formal half bow. "I had to fly in to meet this staff after my board reported such huge earnings from this store. Perhaps you would have dinner with me tonight and tell me some shop secrets of your success."

Lou appeared and nervously shook Conrad McCormick's hand, introducing himself as manager and offering him a tour. As the two started to walk away, I turned to help someone else when Conrad abruptly stopped and said, "I mean it. Dinner. Tonight. 7:00."

"I work until 9:00," I teased.

"Don't care. If you haven't noticed, I own the place. Consider it work. You are going to give me some of your sales tips."

"You are the boss."

He started walking again with Lou, thought of something else, stopped, and turned. "And go pick yourself out a nice new designer dress to wear. You sure are a pretty thing. My driver will pick you up at 7:00 sharp. Be ready. How is Chef's Garden?"

It was a command masked as a question, and he didn't wait for an answer as he turned and walked away. I hadn't been to Chef's Garden in over three years. It was far too expensive, and even before Collier lost his medical license, we only went there for special occasions. My mouth watered at the thought of eating shrimp cocktail and chateaubriand.

G. Keller

Chapter Four

Vivian

Saturday nights at Leo's had become a regular gig. Leo's uncle and his band were usually jamming in the backyard, Leo's dad was the master of the grill, and after the big anniversary party last fall, the twinkle lights remained up, lighting the night sky with the perennial promise of fun. Leo's dad added a brick-paved courtyard for a permanent dancing area, and whoever didn't have plans on a Saturday night, showed up at the Lamont's house. Their place was always electric.

My dad called and was running late on the job site and told me to walk over to the Lamont's without him. He said he would be there in an hour. We lived exactly two blocks from Leo and his family, and I walked over there still wearing my pale blue sundress from my day at Sharon's Riches. Dad said he would bring the French baguette and fresh brewed sun tea, so I didn't have to carry it.

Aside from Leo's charming yellow home, the neighborhood was mostly filled with run-down houses, but since we fixed ours up and Mr. Cooper bought and fixed his house up down the street, and RG Construction was fixing up two other houses, the area now had a feel of newborn life. Several other residents began fixing up their yards and painting their houses. I walked all over the neighborhood now, and it felt safe. It felt like home.

But when I turned the corner and headed to Leo's, a long stretch limo was creeping down the street at a snail's pace. Why would a limo be in this neighborhood? And why was it going so slow? I picked up my pace because I suddenly felt weird. I pretended this out-of-place vehicle was common around here and walked quickly and confidently with my head high. I could tell a window was rolling down. Uh Oh.

"Excuse me, could you point me in the direction of the airport?" An old man asked from inside. He didn't try to lean out the window or make any great effort to show his face.

Instinctively, I knew this was fishy. In today's high-tech world, no one got lost anymore, and certainly the driver knew where to go. We were only a few blocks from the airport and Portofino was not that big. I ignored him and kept walking. I heard a muffled derogatory comment fading away from the cavern of the limo.

I picked up my pace to almost a run. When I reached Leo's yard, I could breathe.

Leo walked out the minute I hit the grass. He was wearing the peace t-shirt I had given him. I ran into his arms, and we kissed. Peace. That is what Leo was to me. Peace.

"Whoa, what did I do to deserve this?" Leo pulled away for a minute and smiled, then kissed me again.

***

Later, when everyone was laughing and eating and drinking and talking, I looked down the long wooden picnic table covered in a red and white checkered tablecloth and was almost full of complete joy. Almost. I knew I couldn't totally feel at peace until I knew where Mom was.

Leo's dad was sitting across from me and Leo, so I bravely asked, "Do you think you could help me find my mom?"

Those sitting within earshot suddenly became quiet. Leo's dad knew the whole story. How mom and dad left on the same day thinking the other one would take care of me—and not knowing both had left. He knew about the notes both of my parents had written to me on that fateful day. He knew about my stealing from

Jewel and her husband to pay the bills, so I could survive on my own. He knew almost everything except for minor details about my bathing and defecating behind bushes. I would take that to my grave. He knew my mom was gone and had already told me that the police wouldn't spend money searching for an adult who left a note explaining their departure.

"I mean, I know the police force can't do an all-out search, but maybe you could help me."

Leo looked at me with concerned sadness, feeling my sorrow and pain.

Leo's dad's voice was rich and deep and full and if you didn't know he was such a nice guy, his voice would sound scary. "Let me see what I can do. Why don't you come by Monday morning, and we can put a plan together. I can ask a detective at the station for a favor. Yes, we will find your mother."

People went back to eating and drinking and talking and laughing and I looked around again thinking, 'Mom, I know you like dressing up and going to fancy restaurants, but you have never experienced this kind of fine dining. Fine food. Fine family. Fine friends.' Real fine dining.

Victoria

"Turn down the next street," Conrad barked to Nestor, his driver and security guard.

"Yes sir."

I was about to ask why he wanted to turn down that dumpy street but knew better. I sat silent.

"Slow down," Conrad said in a tone that turned my stomach.

I looked through the center of the windshield and saw a young girl walking down the street. I hated how he behaved when he saw attractive girls, especially young girls. It just wasn't right. I tried to turn my head and look out the opposite window, ignoring the whole thing because it was so embarrassing, but he started to roll down the window.

What was he doing? This is just…. icky. I wanted to scream at him. I wanted to get as far away from him as possible.

"Excuse me, could you point me in the direction of the airport?"

What on Earth is he doing? He knows where the airport is. I snapped my head so quickly towards the girl and then turned away so she wouldn't see me.

Oh NO! That couldn't have been. It wasn't. She didn't live all the way down here—on this side of town. In this neighborhood. It couldn't have been her. Vivian wouldn't be walking down this street. That just couldn't have been her. It couldn't have been.....

I was forcing my brain to recalibrate. I was forcing myself to disbelieve what I think I just saw. My daughter. In a blue dress. Walking down the street.

The girl ignored Conrad, and he spat, "Bitchy brat. She looked like a younger you."

***

In the beginning......

"Our store carries that dress? Wow! My buyers are good. But I imagine I could put you in a potato sack and you would make it look stunning," Conrad's compliments rolled easily off his smooth tongue.

He held my hand, and I slid into the limousine. I was impressed and in awe at his wealth, having his own driver and limo escorting him everywhere.

He immediately dominated the conversation.

"God, I love coming down here without the wife and kids. Teenagers." He said in disgust. "They are the most ungrateful, spoiled population of people on the planet. I would like to skip over the next decade completely. They make my life miserable, the bastards," he paused, looking me up and down and continued, "I

think I'm going to turn my Portofino home into a bachelor's pad. No wife and kids. Period. They can go to the ranch in Sun Valley. Put a few thousand miles between us." Another pause and leering look. "You don't have kids, I hope. I want to surround myself down here with beautiful, unattached people."

I had taken off my wedding ring before Conrad showed up and put it in my purse. I wanted a night to forget my troubles. I wanted to be someone different for one night. What would it hurt? No one would know about one little night.

"No. No children. No husband. Free as a bird," I smiled seductively.

Just one night.... What could it hurt?

The limo pulled around to the back entrance of the Chef's Garden. "I have a private dining room."

I couldn't believe it. The driver opened the door, and he helped us out of the car. I was so excited that night, living like a rock star when life had been so difficult and depressing. Once in our private dining room, Conrad ordered one delicacy after another..... caviar...... shrimp..... oysters......steak..... and we washed everything down with champagne.

He told me all about his humble beginnings. How he grew up on a farm in Ohio and had to work hard just to help his family put food on the table. How his dad was cold and abusive, and his mom was just as distant and equally mean. How he had six brothers and two sisters, basically bred for free farm labor. When he turned 17, he left the farm and never looked back. He never even went back to visit them. Not once.

He hopped a bus to New York and began working in the garment district, in a factory making coats. He worked hard and learned that when designers didn't sell all their inventory for the season, people could buy clothes at a huge discount during the summer. He saved up enough money to start a discount designer store in New York City where people could buy last year's styles all year long. It was such a success, he began a second, third, and fourth store and then went nationwide. The rest is history. I learned he took his same idea and started discount shoe stores, home goods stores, and discount cosmetic stores.

"You never told your parents of your success?" I asked. "I'm sure they would have been proud of you."

"Nope. I never went back to that disgusting dung heap and never gave them a dime. They put me through hell as a child and didn't deserve my used underwear."

I could tell he was drinking a lot and the conversation was depressing him, so I changed it quickly. "Conrad, you should write a book about your success story. It is fascinating. You are a business genius."

Watching him slowly begin to reignite, I fanned the embers of his enormous ego, eliminating any conversational direction that would bring him unpleasantness. He heatedly responded with grander boasting.

"Oh, you should have seen the crowds that flocked to my first store. I was young and on fire. Nothing could stop me. I knew I had a gold mine on my hands. I had all the top Wall Street hot shots with their fancy business degrees wanting to partner with me. Bullshit rich kids whose parents turned them into cry babies that didn't know what hard work was. They swooned like vultures trying to feed off my sweat. That's what makes a person successful. Sweat. Not some cushy college degree that only taught those snot nosed brats how to get drunk at a frat party and sleep with snooty sorority girls." He paused a moment.

"I bet you were one of those fancy family rich kids. You have that look, but of course you wouldn't be a clerk in my store, I suppose, if you were a trust fund brat."

I didn't want to go down the road of telling too many lies so I gave him the truth about my upbringing. "I was from a normal middle-class family. My dad worked for the city building department, and my mom worked at the mall at the Estee Lauder cosmetic counter.

I guess I fell in love with clothes from going to the mall all the time. My mom was a real beauty. People bought whatever cosmetics she showed them in hopes of looking like her. I had nice parents. Unfortunately, my dad died when I was 13 of a heart attack. He was only 44 and then five years later, my mom got colon cancer and died a year after she was diagnosed. I had no siblings and went to work in the mall, like my mom, right after I graduated from high school." I stopped before the part about helping a young, handsome doctor named Collier find underwear. How Collier made me laugh when he told me he needed ten packs because he hated doing laundry and just threw them away after each use. How he kept coming back to the store for more underwear until he got the nerve to ask me out.

Worried this tale would snuff the heat from the flame I had rebuilt, I smiled and said, "I want to hear more about how you grew your business. I find it so amazing. You really are an incredible rags to riches story. Like in the movies."

Conrad puffed up and proceeded to present a tale of his prosperous expanse across America and how he is now going abroad. At the age of 60, he was twenty years older than me but had the energy of a thirty-year-old. He told me how his stores were going into South America, Asia and then Europe.

When there was a slight break in his tale of conquering the retail world, I said, "I need to be excused," and started to get up from the table to use the restroom.

He grabbed my wrist. Hard. Too hard. Harder than he should have. "I wasn't finished."

"I won't be long. Promise," I winked seductively.

"Don't be." His tone was harsh. I went to the bathroom thinking 'That was a little controlling. No....he just likes me so much. He just had too much to drink. He is just a strong businessman. He just knows what he wants and goes for it. That is why he is successful'....but something wasn't right. I knew it. I refused to acknowledge it. I refused to think about it.

I justified the harshness.

I justified the rudeness.

I justified all of it for a night of fine dining.

***

Why did I lie about not having a daughter? I didn't mean to. It just slipped out. I love Vivian. Why did I say that? And Collier? I loved him, too, once. I loved him deeply. He just made life so hard. His drinking got worse and worse, and I knew it was getting out of control, but I refused to face how bad it was really getting until the accident. Then the problem slapped me in the face and woke me up to the severity of his addiction. I tried to keep it together. I did. I worked and worked and worked, but he just slept. And drank. And slept. And drank. And my resentment grew and grew and grew.

Get a grip Victoria. Stop turning yourself into a victim. You knew what you were doing the minute you slipped off that wedding ring. The minute you agreed to dinner. Business dinner? Right. The way he flirted. The way *you* flirted. You knew exactly what you were doing. Lying. And one lie leads to more lies until you are a daughterless, wifeless prisoner of your own greed.

Chapter Five

Vivian

"Ladies, don't forget that instead of our normal bible study this Wednesday evening, we are having a potluck dinner and guest speaker from Harmony House. We urge you to bring your teenage daughters and friends to this special event. Dinner starts at 5:30 and the speaker starts at 6:30. We hope to see you there." The minister's wife, Allie, announced and then took a seat.

Making God the center of your life is essential to recovering from being an alcoholic. At least, that is part of the 10-step program for Alcoholics Anonymous. When Mr. Cooper took dad into his care last December, going to AA meetings and church were part of the plan, and it was working wonderfully. Dad and I found a church we both liked called Church by the Sea. Each Sunday morning at 10:00 a.m. people gathered at the beach before the crowds filled the sandy shore. There were over 100 people who came to Church by the Sea, setting up beach chairs and blankets, bringing their dogs and coffee and bibles.

Mr. Cooper and Sharon invited us when dad first began his recovery. Leo and his family started to come too, and now, we had a cluster of friends sharing this beautiful experience every Sunday morning. The minister was a nice man who wore a button-down Hawaiian shirt and khaki shorts with flip flops. He was casual and peaceful and gave off an energy of complete calmness and serenity. His gentle smile and smooth voice almost put you into a meditative state as he delivered a universal message of God's love every week.

This church was the polar opposite of the church Mom tried to take me to when dad wouldn't get off the couch. That church was fancy with striking steeples, stained glass, mahogany seating and gorgeous high beamed ceilings. All of Portofino's finest had attended that church and it felt stiff and awkward, more like a fashion show of pretty people. The minister had been nice enough, but Mom just seemed to be going through the motions of attendance. Like if she rubbed her hands on the wooden bench, God would appear like a genie, ready to grant her any wish she wanted to get her out of her depressing situation. And when God didn't behave like a genie in a bottle, Mom stopped attending.

Church by the Sea was so different from the experience I had with Mom. Instantly, I loved that it was at the beach—my favorite place on Earth. I loved gazing out at the blue-green sea while the minister spoke. I loved watching pelicans swoop in the early morning light, careening their wings steadily, angling with precision to scoop up breakfast. I loved watching sandpipers scurry along the foaming wake, searching for a crustaceous meal, dodging the tide with their long stick-like legs.

Admittedly, I'm afraid my love for church was more focused on nature and hanging out with the people I loved most in the world, than it was on God. But as the weeks turned into months of attending Church by the Sea, I began to feel the power of God, and how He can move the unmovable, change the unchangeable, and give power to the powerless. He was giving my dad the strength he needed to resurrect his life, and for that, I was eternally grateful.

I wish church had had the same effect on Mom. I wish she would have felt God's power like Dad did. I wish she could have felt His strength. But she gave up on God, on dad, and on me.

As he did each Sunday, the minister ended by asking everyone to bow their heads and pray. I always prayed for dad to stay strong and thanked Him for bringing my dad back to me and that I had Leo in my life, but today I added another prayer. I thought of dad telling me to forgive my mom. I wasn't ready to forgive her. Her abandonment dug deeper than dad's. I don't know why. It just did. Maybe it was how hard and mean she had gotten the last two years before she left. How cold and distant she had become. Her leaving was really a formality because she had mentally and emotionally left long before that day she taped her goodbye note to my bathroom mirror.

But I didn't like the bitterness bottled up beneath the surface of my skin. I wanted to release the hate, and I just couldn't seem to do it. So, I asked God to help me find her. I needed to ask her why she didn't love me enough to stay. Why she abandoned me. Why money was more important to her than me. I needed to forgive her to stop this feeling, and I thought the only way I could do it was to find her and face her. So that was my prayer today.

God, please help me find my mother. God, please help me find her and forgive her, so I can feel free.

Victoria

I finally got away from Conrad once we reached the beach house and snatched the Portofino Magazine out of my suitcase and slipped into the bathroom and locked the door. I was dying to look at the pictures of our house and read about how it finally got remodeled. As much as I wanted to rip open the magazine, I was frozen looking at the cover. I had such an anguished mixture of emotions. Staring at Collier so happy and healthy looking—a stark contrast from the pathetic passed out drunk he had been for three years. I could hardly remember the last time he looked this handsome.

And Vivian, she was getting so mature looking. She had let her hair go naturally wavy, and it seemed to suit her perfectly. Could this be the girl that passed our limo just minutes ago? I only caught a glimpse. Wavy blonde hair. Blue dress. Walking fast. It could have been her. Conrad had gotten a better look and said she looked like a younger me. Why would she be in that neighborhood walking all alone?

I finally flipped open the pages to find the featured article. I froze when I found the first photo of the renovated interior. The kitchen was spectacular, better than anything I had planned. Gorgeous white shaker cabinets where the folding table had served as our kitchen for the last three years. An infinity marble countertop wrapped the kitchen island and counters. Stainless steel appliances, wide hard wood planked flooring where concrete had been, walls with wonderful modern artwork, a stone fireplace, a beautiful natural wood beam stretching across the kitchen ceiling separated rooms with gothic looking light pendants hanging evenly from it. The lighting was magical, making the room glow, even in a photo.

Each room looked spectacular. And the house was decorated—professionally decorated with furnishings that looked expensive. How did they afford all this? How did Collier finally sober up and get the money to finish it? I began reading fervently. The article focused mainly on the technical high school and how Mr. Cooper and Dr. James were teachers there and created a work-learn program that funded students remodeling homes to learn construction trades. Why was Vivian going to a technical high school? Why was Collier teaching there? How did all that happen?

After obsessively staring at the photos until my mind was temporarily satisfied, I continued flipping through the rest of the magazine like a hypnotized zombie, my mind not really focused on anything as I robotically turned the pages. I almost got to the end when I stopped at a page of advertisements. I just stared.

Thinking. Thinking about it all and trying to digest everything. I wasn't really looking at the magazine anymore. My head was swirling with questions. Then, a tiny photo snapped me into reality. It was an advertisement for Church by the Sea. Dozens of people were gathered on the beach holding bibles. I squinted my eyes to look closer at the photo and there was Collier and Vivian. Standing next to a man in a Hawaiian shirt.

I didn't know how to feel. Cry? Rage? Crumble? Collier must have finally entered a ten-step program. That had to be it. That is how he sobered up. I had begged him to do that for years. I had begged him to go to church with Vivian and me. He wouldn't. He had refused. I didn't really want to go to church, but I read that finding God helped alcoholics reach sobriety, so I went. I found that beautiful Methodist church and took Vivian every Sunday for almost a year. I had hoped he would see us going and join. But he didn't. I finally gave up on the church. And now he was there. At the Church by the Sea. Holding a bible. Sober. Why now? Did my leaving really work? Did it really snap him into being a better father? A better man?

I closed the magazine and hung my head, allowing the tears to slip out, plunk, and splat on the cover, hitting Collier's face. Vivian's face. Distorting the images. Ten steps. He had really done it. He had

45

finally gotten off the couch. He had finally thrown away the booze. He had finally finished the remodel. Why wouldn't he do it for me? Why did he finally accomplish all of this without me? Why couldn't he do the ten steps *for me*?

Chapter Six

Vivian

Another thing I love about going to Church by the Sea on Sunday is that afterwards, everyone stays and has a picnic at the beach. Dad, Mr. Cooper, and Mr. Lamont usually cook something on the park provided grills, the cooler is usually full of ice-cold lemonade and tea, and everyone brings a side dish. We play beach volleyball, swim, build sandcastles, and toss the football.

Only today, no one could stay except Leo and me. Dad and Mr. Cooper were on a deadline with the home they were renovating and had to work all day. Leo and I would help them, but they were solving a roof leak and didn't want us up on a roof. Sharon had extra inventory to organize. Leo's dad had to work at the police station. Leo's mom was taking Leo's little sister and brother to a birthday party and Macy, Leo's other sister, had gotten a job at the hospital and had to work, too. So, it was just Leo and me.

"Vivian," Leo's dad pulled me aside before he left. "I'm off tomorrow. Why don't you come over in the morning, and we will put a plan together to locate your mom."

I smiled and said, "Thank you Mr. Lamont. I appreciate it."

Leo slipped his hand in mine and leaned over to whisper, "I have a surprise for you today."

"Really? What?" We both ambled towards the shore where we had left our blanket and beach bag.

"Let's fold up the blanket. I'm taking you somewhere."

We shook the sand off the blanket and folded it neatly, placing it in my enormous beach bag. Leo grabbed my hand and playfully pulled me down the beach.

"Where are you taking me?" I laughed.

"You will see." Leo pulled me close and kissed me gently. Then he said, "My dad knows the manager of the Beach Club, and he said we could spend the day there. And before you say you don't like fancy things; I need to show you the reason I want to take you there."

We walked a little further down the beach and then up over a white, sandy dune. He unlatched a rod-iron gate and showed the security guard a pass Leo had stashed in his pocket. He pulled a somewhat reluctant me around a corner, and we both stopped in awe.

My mouth gaped and Leo broke the silence, "Now do you see why I brought you here."

This was the most magnificent pool I had ever seen. It had an infinity edge like the one at the point palace where I thought I saw my mother last year, only three times the size. And just like the point palace, the infinity edge looked like it was spilling over into the Gulf of Mexico.

Without another word, Leo let go of my hand, and I threw my bag on an empty chair and dove into the pool. Leo quickly followed.

We popped up near the edge and clung our bodies together under water, with only our head and shoulders visible to the world. Leo began kissing me, and I returned the passion.

"I love you," he whispered between kisses.

"I love you, too," I whispered back.

We let go of each other and began swimming around playfully. After an hour in the beautiful pool and finally exhausted, we got out and flopped on the lounge chairs, moving our beach bags. A waiter came over immediately and asked if we wanted anything.

"Do you have menus?" Leo asked.

"Sure. I'll bring them right over. Would you like a drink?"

"I'll have lemonade," I said.

"Make it two," Leo added.

When the waiter showed up with the lemonade, he handed us two menus and said he would return in a few minutes. I studied the fancy menu.

"I'll take an old-fashioned hamburger. Medium. And fries," I said when the waiter returned.

"Make it two," Leo said and smiled.

"Are you copying me today?" I teased when the waiter left.

"You have great taste," he teased back.

We relaxed on the lounge chairs holding hands in the small space between our chairs. Soon the waiter showed back up with our food and just placed it on the foot of the lounge chairs on trays. I looked at the ketchup in a fancy silver cup and sliced lemons in the lemonade and my mind went back to four years ago when Brianna, Bella, Sarah, Langston, Grady, and Sterling came to the clubhouse at Royal Palm Estates and called me Country Club Girl. That was when Langston told me he loved me. I remember feeling uneasy and awkward when he said it. I remember feeling forced to say it back, so his feelings weren't hurt. I remember the words didn't feel genuine, like he didn't really mean them and neither did I. I couldn't believe I once hung out with them and called them my friends. Thinking back now made me realize that their friendship wasn't the kind of forever friendship I wanted. They weren't authentic. I don't think I ever knew what real friends were like until I went to the tech school. My friends at Lorenzo were different. Kinder. Unpretentious. Real.

I took a giant bite of my burger and looked out across the beautiful blue pool and couldn't believe my eyes. My throat got tight, and I managed to swallow the burger, praying it didn't get lodged in my throat.

There, across the water, sitting on lounge chairs laughing and sipping beverages, were Brianna, Bella, and Sarah and a guy I didn't recognize. What were they doing at the Portofino Beach Club? This was the second time I had seen them in two days. Why were they suddenly hanging out on the south end of town? I thought once I moved away from the north side, I would never have to see that crowd again. But here they were, haunting my happiness.

"This was amazing and thank you so much, but I really want to go back to the beach."

Leo said, "Ok, just let me finish my burger."

I could hardly touch the rest of mine and said, "I need to use the restroom."

I wandered the opposite direction from Brianna and the group, hoping it was the right way to the bathroom and it was. Once inside, I breathed better. I used the bathroom and heard a door open. When I walked out of the stall, I came face to face with Sarah.

"Oh, hey," she said. "I thought I saw you at the pool."

"Hey, Sarah," I tried to sound calm, like I didn't care if I saw her or not, but inside I felt uncomfortable and jumpy. "Do you belong to the Beach Club?"

"No, a friend invited us. Brianna has had a rough couple of months. Her parents split up. I guess her dad was cheating on her mom. It got ugly. Now her mom and dad don't even speak to each other. Then that jerk Langston broke up with her last night. Anyway, she has been a mess and this guy we met invited us here, so we thought it would be fun and take her mind off things."

I didn't really know what to say. "I'm sorry to hear that." There was an awkward pause and neither one of us knew what to say next. A once close friendship with all of them seemed distant and foreign, and I just wanted to leave.

So, I did.

Victoria

In the beginning... ......

After that first dinner at Chef's Garden, Conrad went back to New York....and the flowers began to arrive. Roses. Dozens and dozens of red roses. Almost daily. I didn't know what to do with them. I couldn't take them home. Collier and Vivian would get suspicious. So, I began giving them away to girls at work who began teasing me about how much Mr. McCormick liked me. I told them we were just friends, but no one bought that.

Then the gifts began. Expensive perfume. A diamond bracelet. A sapphire necklace. Conrad began flying into Portofino more regularly to take me to lunch or dinner or both. Then one day, he took me to the Portofino Beach Club where we spent the whole afternoon in the most beautiful suite overlooking the Gulf of Mexico. He ordered champagne and hors' devours to the room and even though I usually don't drink, I drank waaay too much. In fact, every time Conrad came to town, I drank too much. Conrad loved it. I was just trying to escape a little. What could it hurt? No one would know. I had been struggling for so long, a little luxury felt nice.

Then he said, "I want you to be my mistress. I will buy you a breathtaking condo in New York overlooking Central Park. You can buy all the glamorous clothes, shoes, handbags, and jewelry you want. You will travel around the world with me, visiting my stores and meeting with garment makers. With your eye for fashion, you will help influence my worldwide vision for McCormick's. You will attend fashion week in New York, London, and Paris with me. You will travel to exotic destinations, learn new and unique clothing trends, and then help select what McCormick's will buy. You will be at my disposal. I do not plan on divorcing my wife. I need to be clear about that. It will cost me too much money to divorce her. We basically live separate lives. She will not care if I have a mistress. And I will give you everything and more than if you were my wife. You make me feel young and alive. Please say yes."

Before I could answer, Conrad continued, "Think about it overnight. I will be at the airport tomorrow morning early. Pack a suitcase, and I will buy you everything you need from this day forward. If you are not at the airport by 7:30, I will know my answer."

Could I really leave Vivian and Collier? Could I just disappear and never look back? Could I trade in my miserable existence for one that I craved?

Conrad thought I was single with no children. He didn't want more kids. If he knew the truth, he would never want me as a mistress. Maybe, after he couldn't live without me, he would accept Vivian. Maybe after a few months, I could confess I had a daughter, and he would be fine with it. I could launch a fashion career, make big money, have enough to fix the house, divorce Collier, and take back Vivian. It was possible. If Conrad didn't accept Vivian, I would leave him and return home. It would just be a few months.

***

Bam Bam Bam Bam. I jumped, startled.

"Victoria! What the hell are you doing in there?" Conrad began wiggling the doorknob. "Open up. NOW."

I had taken the magazine to the bathroom on Sunday to reread the article and look at the pictures again. Frantically, I looked around for a place to hide the magazine, but the bathroom was stark and sterile, and the linen closet was outside the door. Reluctantly, I opened it.

"Jesus, you were in there forever. What is that?" Before allowing me to answer, Conrad ripped the magazine from my hands. "Is this what you were reading on the plane yesterday? What is so interesting about it?"

Conrad was abusively controlling. It couldn't be that I was just reading a magazine for pleasure. He had to know what I was reading and why.

His eyes squinted as he analyzed the cover. He looked at the people and then me and then back at the cover. He quickly found the article and began speed reading. I racked my brain with a lie to tell him, but out of nowhere, he raised his arm and struck me across the face so hard, I fell to the floor.

"Who are these people? Why do they have the same last name as you? You told me you were an only child, and your parents were dead."

I didn't look at him, nor did I answer.

"WHO ARE THEY?!" He roared.

I thought about telling him they were cousins, but I had told him I had no family here. I was caught, and it was time to tell the truth. The truth I should have told him more than a year ago. The truth that would have saved me from this situation.

Before I had a chance to tell him everything, he struck me again with the rolled-up magazine.

"You lying whore. This girl, Vivian James. Who is she? And this guy," Conrad was fuming as he pointed to the picture. "Who is this guy?" He started beating me with the magazine, his face raging redder and redder as he started spewing offenses. "Tell me the truth! I will find out anyway, so tell me NOW!"

"Yes, Vivian is my daughter and Collier is my husband," I uttered meekly. I felt like I was letting air out of a balloon. The tension letting go, and suddenly I felt relieved to get the truth out of me. The truth. The truth I should have told from the beginning. The truth that had been eating me from the inside. I wanted out of this relationship. I didn't care if I slept on the street. I wanted away from Conrad McCormick. He could beat me one last time, but I was getting out.

Today.

"You told me you weren't married! Are you divorced?" My silence gave the answer.

He began beating me again. "I knew I should have done a background check on you. You are nothing but a lying whore." He kept beating. "What? Didn't he make enough money for you? You thought you would leave him for the high life? You are a pathetic, materialistic bitch. You are nothing but a whore."

I didn't deny anything. He was right. I was no better than a prostitute. I had given myself to a monster for money. He was right about it all.

He stopped beating me and his panting slowed down. He opened the magazine back up and stared and stared. He regained his composure while I laid in fetal position on the floor with my arms covering my head.

"Hey, I recognize her." He paused, still breathing heavily. "Your daughter, Vivian. She was that bitch that wouldn't talk to me when I asked her where the airport was."

I put my arms down and looked at his face. I didn't like what I saw. "So, you left them for me, did you? I bet you just split. Probably left a pathetic note. Couldn't even face them. Didn't even tell them where you were going, did you? You didn't want them to blow your single girl cover." He paused, staring at me, thinking about it all and finally concluding, "Well, you are mine now. And you can never leave. Never. So don't get any ideas."

He threw the magazine at my head, and I didn't even duck. I let it hit me without flinching. My head throbbed and my right arm was sore and probably bruised, but I didn't cry. I was getting just what I deserved. I couldn't deny anything he said. Collier did run out of money. I did just split. I did leave a note. I didn't want my cover blown. I enjoyed the high life...*in the beginning.*

Slowly, Conrad began to get increasingly cruel and abusive. It was like after the thrill of getting me was over, he grew tired of me, almost resenting my existence in his life. One thing that bugged him was that I really didn't like to party. I never was a big drinker. Ever. And when I saw what it did to Collier, I stopped drinking altogether, not even wine with dinner because I thought I could influence him to stop. Conrad hated that I didn't party. That is what he wanted in me—a party girl on the side. In the beginning, I gave him the impression that that is who I was, a party girl. I drank when he wanted me to drink, and he liked it. I knew he did. Why did I act like that? That was not who I am. Why would I pretend to be someone different? Money. That is what it always comes down to. Money. I longed for the luxurious life, and now I loathed it.

All of those promises he made in the beginning about traveling to London, Paris, and Tokyo on fashion trips had lured me into his world, and once he had me, were never mentioned again. When I wanted romance and a relationship, he withdrew and began verbally abusing me, which led to slapping and more. I knew I had to figure out a way to leave and a place to go. I could just walk out and find Collier and Vivian. Would they take me back? Maybe. Maybe not. I could try.

"I'm going to the Beach Club for a meeting," Conrad said sternly. "Repack your suitcases. I'm sending you to my island." He stopped at the door and looked straight at me. "Where you will never leave. No one lies to Conrad McCormick." He swung open the door and said one last chilling thing, "Don't try to run. I'm sending Nestor up to guard the door." And he turned to leave, grabbing my cell phone sitting on the dresser as he walked out the door.

Chapter Seven

Vivian

"We are not finished with our special day. I still have something to give you," Leo slid his arm around my waist as we exited the Beach Club gate and began walking towards the shoreline. "Let's go down to the spot where we first swam together last summer."

We walked leisurely, basking in the sun and salty sea air, quietly content. I wanted to get as far away from the Beach Club and Brianna's gang. Why was I suddenly seeing them all the time? They were a part of my old north side life. The life I left behind. The life where my dad was a drunk and my mom went MIA. The life of rich new money kids who thought they were superior to ordinary people. The life I was so happy to leave.

My new south side life was so different. I loved it. I loved the kids at my school from all parts of Portofino. I loved the cute little houses, Sharon's Riches, the beach. Even the mansions on the south side had an air of time long ago with giant yards and moss-draped oaks and twisted-trunk banyans, undiscriminatingly waiting to shade any sun-drenched soul. These homes were grand, but there wasn't a guard trying to keep you out like so many of the neighborhoods on the north side. Anyone could walk the beach and plop down a chair in the back of one of these castles and enjoy the sand and surf. No guard could tell you to leave.

But why Brianna was suddenly all over the place down here was sort of a mystery. I hadn't seen her since I left Beachside Middle School, except for that one near miss encounter at Sharon's Riches last year when she came to the store with her mom and tried to buy my old dress. Sharon saved the day and told her it was sold. Thank goodness. The thought of her wearing one of my dresses made me sick.

The day of the betrayal, when she posted images of me in the cafeteria with roaches crawling all over my body from my lunchbox explosion, I knew our friendship –whatever friendship we had—was over. Wouldn't a true friend worry about what was going on if your lunchbox was infested with roaches? Wouldn't a true friend reach out to you and see if you were OK? Wouldn't a true friend defend you when others were making fun of you? I would. And my friends at Lorenzo would. Now I wanted her out of my side of town.

Hopefully, that was the last I would see of her for a long time. I didn't plan on going back to the Beach Club any time soon. I see now that she just wanted to be my friend when I was living the country club lifestyle at Royal Palm Estates. Once her free admission to that world was over, she found some new friend to treat her to fancy living. Mom was right about Brianna. She was a user. She used you to get what she wanted. And what she wanted was an expensive existence where she could live like the rich. Mom would know. She was a user too.

"You are deep in thought. Come on. Let's swim," Leo dropped my hand he had been holding. We set our beach stuff down, kicked off our flip flops, and I started to run into the water.

Leo grabbed something in his bag and joined me. We sunk into the sea and both went under, coming up to breathe, wiping the wet from our faces. Leo pulled me close, and we kissed. And kissed. And kissed.

It was getting harder and harder to control the urge to take our kisses to another level. We both felt it and knew these moments were dangerous. His lips tasted salty and wet. His skin against mine electrified me. Our warm breathing got heavy with desire between kisses. I kept my eyes closed, fearing the longing in his eyes, worried I wouldn't be able to control myself. If I kept my eyes closed, I could focus on keeping the electricity harnessed. He pulled back a little and brushed his fingertips lightly, like a feather, across my forehead then gently down my cheek and over my lips. With my eyes still closed, I could feel the love he had for me with his touch. I could sense his intense stare. I risked looking at him. Opening my eyes slowly, his eyes were penetrating my soul with love and desire.

"I have something for you," he whispered, raspy and awkward.

Although we were deep at sea, we could still stand, so I recomposed myself, breaking our locked stare. Leo had a tiny blue velvet box. He opened it, and I was shocked. There was a gold ring with a tiny blue aquamarine stone.

My jaw dropped. "What is this?" I couldn't help but break into a huge smile.

"This is a promise ring. I know I just gave you the charm bracelet, but it isn't enough. My love for you is infinite. I need you to know that. I know our parents would freak out if I gave you an engagement ring, but in my head that is what this is. I am going to be a senior and know exactly what I want to do with my life, build houses, and that life is meaningless without you in it. I know you can't marry me until you turn 18, but I want you to know that the minute you do, I want to marry you. I am so in love with you that the thought of not being with you forever physically hurts," Leo's eyes matched the sky above and twinkled with hope. "With this ring, I promise to always be there for you, always love you, always defend you, always comfort you, always tell the truth, always encourage you, always be your best friend and one day your lover and husband. With this ring, I promise to never stop loving you."

I was wearing the dolphin charm bracelet he had given me, and the ring matched it beautifully.

He slipped the ring on my finger, and I said, "I promise to do all those things, too. Always. I promise. Because I love you too."

Victoria

In the beginning....

As I drove away from the Portofino Beach Club late that afternoon, Conrad's words ponged inside my head, "I promise to completely take care of you, so you won't have to worry about anything. I promise."

Not having to worry about money was like a heavy weight being lifted from my shoulders. Worry had become my albatross, keeping me from finding peace and joy.

"You won't have to worry about anything," he said. "I promise."

Chapter Eight

Vivian

"What is the exact date and time your mom left you the note?"

Mr. Lamont was sipping coffee at his kitchen table, pen in hand, ready to write down my answers on a yellow legal pad. "April 10th, a year and two months ago."

"Tell me about that day," he asked.

"It was early. About 6:30 in the morning. I thought it was weird because she usually made loud noises in the morning, sort of encouraging everyone to get up, but not that morning. She was extra quiet. I was in bed still sleeping. I barely heard her leave."

"But you did hear her leave?"

"Yes. Then I went to the bathroom and saw a letter taped to the mirror." I pulled the letter out of my backpack to show him.

He looked at it closely and took out his phone. "Do you mind if I take a picture of it?"

I shook my head no.

"Did you try to call her?"

"Yes, but the phone went to voicemail and the mailbox was full. Later in the day I was notified that the bill needed to be paid. Then it shut down completely."

"Where did your mom work?"

"McCormick's Department Store."

"Did you ever call them and ask where she was?"

"I did. The person on the phone said she just quit. No one knew where she went."

"Tell me some thoughts about why you think she left."

"Well, dad hadn't worked in three years and that made mom mad. She yelled at him a lot at first, but the last few months she was just silent. She hardly spoke. She never smiled. She just seemed to be robot-like. Just going through the motions. She hated being poor. She liked nice things and not having the house remodeled for three years, with no real end in sight, was making her miserable. I wasn't totally surprised she left. I kind of figured their marriage wasn't going to survive, but I thought she would tell me herself. Not in some note. And I never thought she would just disappear. Divorce.

Yes. I thought my parents would divorce, but never just leave without a trace."

Leo's dad was writing as I spoke.

"Then last June I was walking past the airport and stopped to watch the planes land and take off, and I am pretty sure I saw her boarding a private jet with an older man."

"Do you remember the day?"

"Yes, it was June 17th at about three in the afternoon." That day was burned in my memory. "She also left her driver's license and social security card in one of her purses she didn't take. I thought that was weird. Doesn't a person need a driver's license? I thought maybe she just forgot it because it was in one of her favorite purses. I had hoped she would come back for it, but she didn't."

"Hmmm. I can check to see if she applied for a new one. I can also check the airport log and see who was flying out that day. I don't think it should be too hard to find her if she didn't change her name and wasn't trying to disappear," said Mr. Lamont and he took a photo of her license and social security card.

Victoria

In the beginning……

I sat on the chair facing a passed-out Collier, thinking about our last conversation. The one where he said he didn't have a problem. The one where he said he could stop anytime. The one where he said he would stop tomorrow —but tomorrow came and went and came and went, and he hadn't stopped drinking.

Staring at him now, like this, sickened me. His beard was long and matted and his skin hung loose on his bones like oversized wet clothes on a child. This saggy skin gave him an appearance of being much older than he was. And he was so handsome…. once upon a time. Once upon a time, he was dashing in a suit and tie, clean shaven, and happy. He was happy once, wasn't he? We used to laugh and go to movies and hold hands and kiss. We were so in love…. once upon a time.

What happened to us? Why did he start to drink so much? Why didn't he love me enough to change? Why wouldn't he admit he had a problem? He used to love me. He did. He told me all the time how I was the best thing that ever happened to him. That he was so proud of me. That he loved being my husband. What changed? We could say it was the incident where he operated on his patient's wrong eye and blinded him, got sued, and lost his medical license, but we both knew the dissipation of our marriage began before that. His drinking began before that.

I couldn't remember the last time we laughed or held hands or kissed. Looking at him like this, drunk and passed out, like a bum under a bridge, turned my stomach. I couldn't imagine this creature happy. He seemed so pathetic, so repulsive. I didn't recognize him. This creature took over my husband and sucked all the life out of him. I wanted to believe him when he said he could quit drinking. In fact, I believed him over and over and over.

As I continued to stare, my eyes caught a glimpse of the corner of a wine box peeking out from under the sofa. I got up to throw it away and when I did, I lifted the flap along the base of the couch to grab it and saw another wine box. I got down on my knees and looked under the sofa. Dozens of empty wine boxes were littered in his dark hiding place. I stood back up, dropping the box I was holding, letting it clunk on the floor. Collier didn't even flinch. I would think he was dead if it wasn't for the faint movement of his chest, letting small amounts of air in and out. His body was alive, but whatever we once had was dead.

I thought of kissing him one last time, but what was the point? It may stir him awake and then what? Another conversation about how he could stop drinking if he wanted to? More lies about restarting his life? Another pointless talk dragging out the obvious end of this relationship?

I remember one of our first official dates. We went to see Fleetwood Mac in concert in Tampa. We both had so much fun and had so much in common. We loved the same music and shouted the lyrics to songs like 'Monday Morning', 'Don't Stop,' and 'The Chain'. I remember him holding my hand for the first time and whispering, 'I will never break the chain.' He kissed me, and I could see the love in his eyes, unlike any guy I'd ever dated. I knew that night he was the one.

Now, I couldn't even kiss him goodbye.

I turned and walked away. Away to pack. Away from this gutted, kitchen-less, floor-less, wall-less cavern. Away from this broken marriage. Away for good.

It was the only solution I could think of. If he had to care for Vivian. If he had to be the provider. If he had to be in charge. Maybe-- just maybe-- he would stop drinking.

And if I stayed, he would continue to depend on me to handle everything. And everything wasn't being handled. I couldn't keep up with the bills. I just couldn't. I appeared to be doing alright, but underneath, I had stopped taking care of everything. I had gotten so overwhelmed. I just shut down inside. I just couldn't do this anymore.

Leaving Vivian would be the hardest. Could I do it? I opened her bedroom door slightly and stared at her beautiful face. I held in tears and gently closed the door. One day, I would return and explain—I told myself. Then I slipped into her bathroom and taped the note to the mirror, lifted my suitcase, and walked out.

I drove my car to the dealership where I bought it and left it in the parking lot with a note attached and keys in the ignition. I was four months late on payments and knew they would be taking it back soon anyway. I arranged a cab to pick me up and take me to the airport.

"I knew you would come," a seductive smile spread across his face, and he wrapped his arms around me. We kissed.

"Oh no, I switched purses and forgot my driver's license."

"Don't worry. I fly by private jet. You won't need one. You can apply for a new license in New York, your new hometown."

And just like that, I flew away....

Chapter Nine

Vivian

All the new inventory was organized, recorded, and displayed in the store. With nothing more to do and Sharon at the bank, I got out the sketch pad and drawing pencils my dad bought me as a gift for selling the house in Royal Palm Estates. He said I could have anything I wanted, and I chose art supplies.

I had fallen in love with art and design and thought maybe I wanted to be an architectural engineer one day. I had this fantasy of designing cottage style tiny homes on beautiful, treed lots with white picket fences. I didn't think that because you couldn't afford a giant house, your home had to be dumpy looking.

In my free time, I sketched exterior images of cottage homes. I would add flower boxes, banyan trees, a fence, sometime a dog in the yard. I also loved designing infinity pools and would color them in with various shades of blue colored pencils.

Another drawing obsession I had was furniture designing. When we were renovating the rest of our old house in Royal Palm Estates, I loved learning how to use the bandsaw. The smell of freshly cut wood gave me comfort and peace. I loved working with my hands, creating something purposeful and beautiful. So, when I wasn't drawing houses, I was usually drawing sofas, tables, chairs, lamps, and cabinets.

Today, I was not in the mood to draw houses or sofas, so I started sketching and designing something different—clothes—and I was having quite fun with it. When I was dressing one of the mannequins earlier, I thought of a casual line of teen clothes that were understated, yet classy, and not expensive. I thought it would be nice if girls could buy clothes that looked good but cost less.

Once I began, the ideas fired in my brain faster than I could draw.

Sharon walked in and asked, "What are you drawing?"

I showed her and she said, "These are cool."

"Just having some fun," I said finishing a sketch of some willowy striped pants.

"I have a treat for you today," Sharon said. "We are going to close the shop for a two-hour lunch break and head over to Saks Fifth Ave to shop and have some lunch. My treat. I like to go to Saks a few times a year to see the latest fashions and get an idea of retail pricing. I also like to see how they style their mannequins. It can inspire ideas."

Even though I hated the exclusivity of the Waterford Shopping Plaza, the idea for inspiration was intriguing. I could get ideas to sketch some clothes. I closed my sketch pad and followed Sharon out the door.

***

When we entered Saks Fifth Avenue, the smell of money permeated the air. Everything about this store was laced with expense. The glittering chandeliers, the polished white tile flooring, the mirrored cosmetic counters, the salespeople in posh clothing, were all a prelude to a very expensive price tag. I picked up a cool looking shoe and turned it over. $1,345! I quickly put it down.

Mom used to love coming in here to shop when I was little. I had no idea this was how much she was spending. It was ridiculous when you think about it. Why would a person feel the need to spend this kind of cash on a pair of shoes? I was happy in my $19.95 pair of white sneakers from Target.

"Sharon!" exclaimed a very slick man in a pale pink suit and a freshly cut and greased pompadour hairstyle.

The two embraced and gave each other a kiss on each cheek.

"Arnie! So good to see you!" Sharon seemed genuinely happy to see this man.

"Arnie, this is my assistant, Vivian. We are here to check out your latest styles. I need to see what to charge my customers when your clothes end up in my shop after one or two wears," Sharon winked smiling, and Arnie smiled back.

"Vivian, you are precious. Where did you find this young beauty, Sharon? I want to steal her for my store and just have her walk around in fine clothes. I would sell thousands," Arnie was giving me an up and down approval that was meant to be funny not crude.

"Vivian, Arnie and I go way back. We went to school together at Portofino High before he went to the Fashion Institute in New York and became Saks Fifth Avenue's number one buyer and then manager of this store," Sharon explained.

"Yes, Sharon saved me from going out of my mind in that prison they called school," Arnie twirled his eyes and said, "You girls have fun looking around and let me know if you need help."

"Good to see you, Arnie," Sharon smiled warmly.

"You too, love," and he blew her a dramatic kiss, backing slightly away, and was about to turn when a sophisticated older man appeared out of nowhere.

"Conrad!" squealed Arnie. Arnie gave another dramatic hug.

Standing right behind this older man was Brianna. *What was going on?* Was this her grandfather? Sharon and I stood awkwardly. I wanted to exit this encounter in the worst way, but Sharon stood smiling, and I realized it would be impolite.

"Sharon, this is Conrad McCormick. He owns McCormick's Department stores, along with Pearls Fine Jewelry, Penny Saver Shoes, Roll Back Home Goods, just to name a few. He comes in here from time to time to do the same thing as you. Scout the fine goods. He then buys last year's styles at a discount for his stores. Conrad, Sharon owns a charming secondhand retail shop called Sharon's Riches."

Arnie's brain seemed to be firing on all cylinders and if this were a cartoon, a light bulb would have popped up over his head. "Oh my, I have an excellent idea. I am hosting a charity event at the Beach Club this Friday. It is a fashion show put on by retailers in the area. The money from everything we sell will go to the Homeless Shelter of Portofino. Apparently, this is a big problem right now in Portofino. All kinds of people living in the Everglades." Arnie shivered dramatically—everything Arnie did, he did dramatically. "You both must be a part of this. I won't take no for an answer."

Conrad McCormick was smooth and charming, but there was something about him that gave me an uncomfortable feeling. Mom had worked at McCormick's. I wonder if she ever met him. Then suddenly, I realized something, and every hair stood on the end of my skin. I think this was the creep in the limo that tried to ask me for directions to the airport. I think. I can't be sure because I didn't really get a good look at him, but the voice was eerily familiar. Why was Brianna hanging out with him? Why was he lurking in my neighborhood, pretending to ask for directions? It was obvious now that he was in Portofino a lot and certainly knew where the airport was. I got this icky feeling in my stomach and wanted away from this guy.

He smiled and said, "If these two beauties are going to be a part of it, then I definitely want McCormick's to be represented." He was staring at me with a leer that suggested he remembered me, but he didn't bring up the encounter.

I wanted to pull Sharon away and shout no, but the Homeless Shelter of Portofino was my charity. The charity that I was dedicating a percentage of proceeds from RG Construction to help. Sharon knew this and enthusiastically said, "We would love to help that charity! Right Vivian?"

Reluctantly, I said, "Yes, that would be nice."

Arnie said, "Fabulous! Here is my card." He pulled out two cards and handed the cards to Sharon and Mr. McCormick. "Call me tomorrow and I'll go over details with you."

Brianna, who had been silent through the whole exchange, suddenly caught Sharon's eye. I could tell Sharon recognized her.

This familiarity caught Arnie's attention, too, and he turned to Brianna and said, "Do you know each other?"

I broke the awkwardness and admitted, "Yes, Brianna and I went to elementary and middle school together."

I couldn't quite figure out the look in Mr. McCormick's eye. This seemed to please him, which made me more uncomfortable. "Brianna works at our store on the north side of town. She is one of my best employees. I am treating her to a shopping spree today for being such a hard worker."

I saw the packages Brianna was holding. She had this fake arrogant look on her face, and I thought this whole thing seemed fishy.

Sharon glanced at me and probably saw how uneasy I was feeling and took the cue, "Well, nice meeting you. Enjoy your day."

"Bye," I said and couldn't get away fast enough.

***

After browsing both the adult and teen sections of Saks, Sharon suggested we go lunch someplace else. We ended up at this little local dive that had amazing fresh fish tacos and a lively hum of people.

Feeling more comfortable, I decided to share my feelings about Brianna and what happened Saturday with the limo and Mr. McCormick. Sharon agreed it was strange and an older man like Conrad McCormick shouldn't be hanging out and buying Brianna gifts nor should he be asking a young girl on the street for directions.

"You should call her and tell her it isn't a good idea to take gifts from him or hang out with him alone," Sharon suggested.

"I don't even talk to her anymore. She has this weird idea that she somehow has to impress me with how she can afford expensive stuff now. Like when she came in and bought that dress in your store and pulled out all that cash. I guess she could have made money working at McCormick's, but it all seems so.... sketchy."

Sharon agreed. "Maybe you should call her mom and tell her."

"It wouldn't do any good. She would think I'm trying to hold her back from luxury living. It would probably make her want to spend more time with that creep. Besides, I don't even have her number anymore. I lost it when I switched phones," I paused a moment, thinking about Brianna and this weird situation. "I guess I could talk to her at the fashion show, if she is there."

"I think that is a good idea. I can talk to her, too, if you want," Sharon added. "She might listen more if an adult talks to her."

"Maybe. Brianna and I used to be best friends in elementary school. We did everything together—we slept over at each other's house, went to movies, the beach, roller skating, everything. Then, when I moved into Royal Palm Estates and started middle school, things started to get weird. She loved hanging out at our country club, was obsessed with what I wore, and then took my boyfriend away. It started to feel like she was in competition with me, but I didn't really know it at the time."

"There are a lot of girls like Brianna. Women too. Always in competition to have the best. That is why my business does so well, but it is kind of sad, isn't it? Well, you are right. She should not be hanging out with Mr.

McCormick. You have good instincts, Vivian. That situation is definitely sketchy."

Victoria

Nestor kept the glass partition in the limo closed, so I couldn't talk to him. I was stunned that Conrad had taken my cell phone the minute he found out Vivian was my daughter, and I was still married to Collier. For over a year, I could have called someone and left him, but I didn't. Now, I had no way of contacting help and was heading for a remote island with a security guard. Basically, prison.

I thought of screaming when Nestor deposited me onto the jet, but Conrad's final words last night were chilling, "If you make a scene at the airport, I will find your daughter. You don't want me to do that now, do you?"

How could I not see what kind of monster he was in the beginning? How many red flags were flown in front of my face? His constant self-promotion. His dictator dominance. His lack of caring for anyone other than himself and his own ambitions. His off-handed put downs. His need to control. Had I not seen all of this before running away with him? Why would I want to be a prisoner to him? Was I that desperate? Was I that pathetic? What was wrong with me walking so willingly into his trap?

The jet took off, and I felt despondent, defeated. I closed the window shade and closed my eyes, but I was too restless to sleep and kept fidgeting in my seat. I stared into the space in front of me and my old art pad was sticking out of the magazine rack. I reached over and grabbed it. I hadn't picked up this notebook in several months. When Conrad first convinced me to be his mistress, I told him I once dreamed of being a fashion designer. He bought me a sketch pad and told me to start drawing. He told me he knew all the major designers in New York-- that he could get me discovered. He was so convincing. I believed him. I had wanted a different life so badly that I believed the lies.

I thumbed through the notebook looking at all those sketches.... all those fantasies.....all those big dreams. What a fool I was. Thinking I was going to be this big shot designer. Thinking Conrad was really going to introduce me to Vera Wang or Marc Jacobs. Thinking I was good enough to be taken seriously. I ripped out a page and tore it to shreds, watching the once hopeful sketch float like confetti to the floor.

I couldn't take this life anymore. I was worn out. Living with a drunk Collier wore me out. Living with an abusive Conrad wore me out. Mental exhaustion leads to terrible decision making, and I can't take it anymore. I have made way too many weary, bad decisions and now, I'm about to become convicted of my own sins. If Conrad thinks he is going to keep me on this island like a prisoner, he is grossly mistaken. No man is determining my fate anymore.

I knew what I was going to do. I was done with this world. I was done with Conrad. I was done with Collier. I was done being poor. I was done being rich. I was just done. Vivian would be OK. She was strong. Stronger than me. She wouldn't fall for a monster like Conrad. She wouldn't let him manipulate her. She was a survivor. I saw how confident she looked on that magazine cover. I saw how she managed to help finish the remodel, how she got her dad to sober up. Yes, Vivian was a strong survivor. Unlike me.

I stared out the jet window, suddenly hypnotized by the shades of blue, and decided that when we landed, I was going to take a swim. A swim out to sea. An endless swim. A swim to set me free.

The jet landed and came to a screeching halt. I stood, grabbed my bag, and dropped the sketchpad on the seat, turning away from the broken dreams.

G. Keller

Chapter Ten

Vivian

"Hello, Vivian. I have some news for you," Leo's dad's baritone voice bellowed as he got out of his police car.

I had just gotten home from Sharon's Riches and was watering the flower boxes. I anxiously turned off the hose and wiped my hands on my shorts.

Mr. Lamont walked across the lawn with a somber face and said, "I went to McCormick's Department store and found a clerk who worked with your mom. She said Conrad McCormick, the owner of the store, took a liking to her and started sending her flowers and gifts. Then one day, she told a coworker she was quitting and moving to New York. She said she got a job at one of McCormick's stores there. I also went to the airport to investigate the times and destinations of private jets. It looks like your mom left for New York with Conrad McCormick on the day she left you the note, and on the day you saw her at the airport, they had been in town for a few days. I also checked records in New York. Your mom got a driver's license there and an apartment. The apartment is registered under a corporation name. I researched the corporation, and it belongs to Conrad McCormick. It looks like she ran away with him."

Leo's dad paused as he watched me digest this information. Then he hesitated with his next news, "One more thing. McCormick's plane is here, and records show your mom is here with him now. I found an address for him in Olde Portofino down by the pier. She is most likely staying there right now with Mr. McCormick."

My mind began to swim. Conrad McCormick. Owner of McCormick's Department Store. That creepy old dude with Brianna. The one who drove by in the limo and asked me for directions. Why would mom go off with *him*? I had to see her. Now. It couldn't wait. I had to face her. I had so many questions I needed answers to. Like how could you abandon me? How could you leave me to survive alone with no food or water or electricity? Why did you love money more than me? Why would you leave dad for such a gross, old man?

"What is the address?" My voice quivered.

Mr. Lamont handed me his business card with the address on the back. "Why don't I drive you there tomorrow?"

Looking down at the address with tears filling my eyes, I muttered, "Thank you, but I don't know if I'm ready yet. Can I have a day to think?"

He gave me a hug and said, "Sure, honey. Are you alright?"

"Yes. I'm fine."

But I wasn't fine. I wasn't alright. I was the opposite of alright. And I wasn't going to wait a day to think. This confrontation needed to be done now and alone, without dad or Leo's dad. I needed her to answer my questions. I needed her to look me in the eye and tell me why she abandoned me.

Victoria

In the beginning…….

"I want to fly you to my private island," Conrad murmured breathlessly into my ear.

"You have a private island?" I asked impressed.

"Yes, and the only people there are the maid and butler, a husband-and-wife team, who keep it ready for

when I want to entertain. And I want to entertain you."
He kissed me on the neck.

*And just like that we were boarding his jet and
flying from New York, where he had just purchased me a
beautifully decorated and furnished condo overlooking
Central Park, to a remote island in the Caribbean.*

How could I have thought that one day this island
that I was so impressed with was going to be my prison?

"Are you alright?" Maxwell, the island manager
who I had only met once, asked.

Why didn't I tell him no. Why didn't I tell him
Conrad was a monster? Why didn't I beg for help?

Why?

Because I didn't deserve help. I was embarrassed
that I had fallen for someone like Conrad. I was too
humiliated to face Vivian and Collier--to confess what a
horrible thing I did, leaving them for such a cruel person,
leaving them for money. Let's face it. I was no better
than a prostitute.

My body felt weak, like I could hardly lift a limb.
My brain felt dull and vacant of emotion. My desire to
go on was gone. Soon my pain would be over.

Chapter Eleven

Vivian

"Hey, Dad. I'm going to meet some friends for sunset at the beach, and then we are going to Third Street Coffee," I lied. I had never lied to my dad. Ever. But I didn't want him to know I was going to confront Mom. I didn't want him to come. I needed to do this alone. He would understand after. I would tell him the truth then.

And because I had never lied to him, he believed me without question. "Ok. Cooper, Leo and the boys are helping me finish some trim work and we will be late anyway. Have fun."

I didn't want to call Leo. I didn't want him talking me out of this. No one was going to stop me from seeing her. No one.

Right now, I was only thinking about confronting Mom. Nothing else could penetrate my thoughts. My mind was too busy going over questions I was going to ask her, and my stomach was fluttering with energy.

I googled the address and saw that it was only 20 minutes away by bike. I shoved my phone in my small backpack, strapped it on and grabbed my bike from the garage.

I ignored traffic lights and barely slowed down while looking both ways to see if cars were coming. Once down in Olde Portofino, I stopped on a quiet tree-lined avenue to check my phone GPS. Being that the mansions in Olde Portofino were on city streets and not in gated communities like on the north side of town, I could easily zoom in on the street view of McCormick's mansion. I was only two blocks away.

I rode slowly now. The sun was setting, and the sky cast a burnt orange blanket over the seaside town, slowly snuffing out the daylight. My heart was beating loudly in my chest. How would mom react when she saw me? Would she be shocked? Mad? Happy? Embarrassed? How was I going to react? Shocked? Mad? Happy? Embarrassed?

My heart wouldn't quiet as I swung my leg over the bike seat and gently stepped on the meticulously manicured lawn. The house was grand, but not on the beach like Jewel's and Charlotte's mansions. This one was on the bay, across the street from the beach, and I'm sure a large yacht was docked in the backyard.

Now or never. I walked up the stone steps with false bravado and pounded ferociously then stepped back slightly. I waited. And waited. Again, I pounded. Stepped back. Waited. No one came to the door. I peered through the glass panels that flanked each side of the giant wood door. Not a stir. I looked around. No car in sight. Garage door closed. I looked again through the windows. Lights were off inside, and everything was getting increasingly darker.

I'm not sure what got into me, but the old Roach Girl from last year came to life, and I slipped quickly down the stone steps and pulled my bike behind a hedge, out of sight. Then I whisked around the side of the mansion to the back where there was a stone wall with a rod iron gate, almost identical to the one outside my parents' bedroom patio in Royal Palm Estates.

Without thinking of the ramifications, I tried the gate door, but it was locked. So, I easily hurdled the gate, landing on both feet like I had done last summer when this was my routine for entering and exiting my old house. I tried the back sliding doors. The first two were locked, but the third one slid right open. If an alarm went off, I planned on slipping back out and disappearing down the street on my bike. But luckily, no alarm. I cannot believe these rich people leaving their doors unlocked. Once in, I looked around at the enormous home and realized......mom got what she wanted. The luxury life she was missing the last three years with dad.

I don't know why I broke into the house. I guess I wanted to see what was so special about this place. Why she would want to trade in me for this. I wandered around sort of in an aimless curiosity, boldly analyzing the paintings, the furnishings, the architectural details. There was a sculpture on a pedestal. It was a smooth, stone image of a person, not male or female. Sort of abstract. What made me linger was the clunky chain link necklace around the neck of the smooth stone human image. The chain was grossly larger than the person could possibly bear, and the androgynous creature was hunched over with the burdened weight of it.

I unknowingly made my way to the owner's suite, mom's new bedroom I presumed. It was grand. A king bed with gold and white luxurious bedding and pillows, windows with magnificent views of the bay and yes, there was the yacht. I peered into the bathroom that was more like a hotel spa. Marble. Crystal. Gold. Grand.

I opened the door of the closet that was at least double the size of my bedroom. In the middle was a giant island cabinet. I pulled open a drawer. Underwear. Another drawer. Bras. I walked the row of designer clothing running my hand along the sleeves as I passed.

Then I stopped and noticed that many of the clothes still had tags on them.

My mind flashed to the wardrobe box mom left behind when she abandoned me. The box that was filled with new clothes. Clothes with expensive tags. Clothes that were never worn. Rage surged over me like a tsunami, pulling rational thoughts out to sea with its strong undertow. Nothing could save these thoughts from the powerful surge. Fury. Just like last year when I discovered mom's addiction to shopping. She couldn't stop. This is why she was with Conrad McCormick. Gown after exquisite gown. Shoes. Jimmy Choo. Bergdorf Goodman. Neiman Marcus. Thousands of dollars in shoes. Thousands of dollars in gowns.

Hate stung my eyes making them water. My chest heaved while I desperately tried to control my breathing. Calm down, Viv. Calm down. Get control. Deep breaths. Eyes closed.

Suddenly, I had an idea. An idea I couldn't control. An impulsive, brilliant idea. I was going to take a designer dress. A dress to be auctioned off at the charity fashion show this Friday. I began rummaging through the gowns until I found one with a price tag of $4,876. It was a pink strapless tea length formal gown with giant chiffon flowers gathered all over the skirt. It was exquisite. A showstopper. A one-of-a-kind dress that would stand out in a fashion show. I grabbed a pair of shoes, Jimmy Choos-probably a couple of grand, that would look elegant with the pink gown. I opened my small backpack and regretted not bringing my larger one. There was no way this dress would fit. I contemplated finding a different dress but didn't want to take the time. I quickly shoved the shoes in the backpack.

Now, I had the urge to get out of there fast. I went from wanting to confront Mom to wanting to flee, like a roach whose dark adventure just ended with a bright light switch.

I started to exit the bedroom when I heard a door open and laughter echo in the foyer.

Scurrying, I found an escape through a cracked open door that led to a hall closet. I burrowed way back behind coats and jackets, barely breathing. How was I going to get out?

The laughter got louder. I tried to discern the voices, but no one was talking, just giggling. I didn't recognize my mom's laugh at all. In fact, I knew it wasn't mom. But there was something recognizable about the laugh.

"Did you have fun shopping? See, I told you my store had just as nice of things as Saks. That's why people love shopping at my stores. Great clothes. Great price. I make so much more money than Saks Fifth

Avenue. Last year, my stores' earnings were triple what Saks were." He stopped bragging for a moment and then continued. "I want you to model the dresses for me. You need practice if you are going to represent McCormick's at the fashion show next weekend."

Brianna. It had to be.

Mr. McCormick.

Why was she here alone with this guy? And where was Mom?

Victoria

Maxwell brought my bags to my suite and set them down. I wasn't even planning on changing into a bathing suit. What was the purpose of that when all I wanted to do was drift out to sea? Prolonged disillusionment had led me to utter despair. There was no way out. I couldn't shake the depression. Once I made the decision to float my worries away, a motherly peace wrapped her arms around my entire body in a tight embrace. I felt snug, protected, calm...... for the first time....... in so long.

I sat on the bed and laid my head for a moment on the pillow. I was so tired. So so tired.

Vivian

After what seemed like hours of modeling clothes, I heard the laughter diminish, so I cracked open the closet door. The back door closed, and the voices stopped. They must have gone back by the pool. I quickly slipped out the front door and ran to my bike. Folding the fluffy gown, I carefully laid it in the bike basket.

Suddenly, I heard the front door open, and I pulled my bike back further out of view.

"I really need to go home now, Mr. McCormick. My mom is expecting me," Brianna was loud, and her voice sounded uneasy and a little desperate. I don't think I have ever heard Brianna's voice sound nervous. She was definitely nervous.

"Ok. Ok. But you need to practice modeling all those clothes. Friday will be here soon."

I heard car doors open and close. Then I saw limousine taillights exit the circular driveway.

I was about to get on my bike and speed home. It was completely dark, and my dad may be home by now.

I had put my phone on silent before I left and was sure there were a few messages from Leo.

But before I mounted the bike, I stopped. I stared at the bike basket. I bet it could hold one or two more gowns. I could quickly slip in the house again through the back sliding door unless Conrad locked it. I could take two, maybe three more dresses that were not as puffy as this one. It somehow felt like the revenge I needed. Mom shouldn't have left me for money. She shouldn't have. I could take away her greed and give it to those who needed help. I bet I could raise over ten thousand dollars for the homeless shelter with just a few of her ensembles.

She owed the homeless.

She owed me.

For over a year she didn't try to contact me once. But she had time to shop.

With a resurgence of anger, I didn't hesitate another moment. I leaned the bike against the bushes and slipped again behind the house, grazed the gate, and like a professional thief, checked the same slider. Sweet. Still open. Seconds is all it took for me to select three more magnificent gowns with matching shoes. I hope she is at the fashion show on Friday. I can't wait for her to see me walk out in one of her gowns. I know they will fit. I have grown into her exact size. In fact, when she sees me, she will be shocked at how I look exactly like her. But I don't act like her. I am the opposite of her. I would never trade my daughter for a $4,000 gown.

Unlike last summer when I stole the money from Jewel, I had absolutely no remorse stealing from mom. Mom left me. Mom left Dad. Mom hasn't had to suffer like I had to last year. She has been living the luxury life. Mom owes me these gowns. She owes the charity that supports the homeless shelter these gowns.

I slipped out the front door and picked up my bike. I carefully folded the clothes and put them in the basket with the shoes laying on top. As I mounted my bike, I heard a door slam at the house next to McCormick's, making me hustle away and out of sight. Away from that horrid house of unnecessary opulence.

Victoria

Rap Rap Rap......RAP RAP RAP**.....RAP RAP RAP**....... "Victoria......Are you in there?" I felt like I was underwater trying to pull myself to the surface, but there was this ball and chain pulling me back down.

Who was calling my name?.......Vivian?....... Collier?........ God?.........

My head was heavy. My mind was cloudy. I couldn't think or focus. Where was I? Did I go out to sea? That was my plan. Did I do it? I was trying to remember but couldn't think straight.

I managed to mumble, "Yes, I'm coming." I realized I wasn't out to sea. For a moment, I thought I was floating in heaven. But I wasn't. I was very much still on Earth. I barely remember flying to the island last night. Then coming to this room. Everything was getting clearer now that I was waking up.

I must have fallen asleep before I had a chance to drift to sea.

The voice must be Maxwell. I slowly walked to the door in a daze. When I opened it, Maxwell was holding a phone with an urgent look on his face.

"It's Mr. McCormick."

I took the phone. "What the hell took you so long?"

"Sorry, I was asleep."

"There has been a change in plans. I need you back here tomorrow. I have signed McCormick's Department Store up for a charity event Friday night. I want you to run the event. You might be a pathetic whore, but you have good taste and can make sure the store is represented well."

I could say no. What could he do? Beat me up from across an ocean?

Or I could say nothing at all. Or just say Ok. Then once off the phone, follow through with my plan to go out to sea.

"Ok," I went with the path of least resistance.

"I'll have my jet there to pick you up tomorrow. That will give you a couple of days to plan outfits for some young models I found. In fact, you may know them. They are friends of your daughter," Conrad paused while I tried to make sense of what he was saying. "They are cute girls. Of course, not as pretty as your daughter. I met her today. Vivian, isn't that her name? Beautiful. *Very* beautiful. She looks like a *very* young you."

I handed the phone back to Maxwell and closed the door. I walked in a daze and sat on the edge of the bed, staring blankly at the white wall. A slight movement from the bottom corner of the wall snapped me out of my trans-like state.

A large roach, once slightly moving but now frozen from being spotted, was also contemplating his next move. Boldly, he decided to skirt across the blank wall, totally exposed in the dangerous light, totally risking being destroyed, totally unafraid of what the future held for him.

I used to be afraid of roaches. It was something Vivian and I had in common. Just the sight of them sent us screaming like we were about to be murdered. I wonder if she was still afraid of them. If she ran and screamed when she saw one.

I watched that large roach find his way clear to the other side of the wall, down the corner, along the baseboard and out the crack under the door. He made it. No shoe smashed his body. No spider web snared his limbs. No spray snuffed out his life sending him freefalling to the floor.

I didn't scream. I didn't run. I didn't flinch. I just watched him escape. Unharmed. For now, anyway.

Chapter Twelve

Vivian

Riding my bike home in the dark with a basket full of stolen clothes was an out of body experience. If someone had told me two years ago that this is where I would be at this very moment, I would have told them they were insane. But here I was, racing across streets like I was in the Tour de Force. I planned on just riding home at a normal speed to not draw attention to myself with stolen clothes in a basket, but I saw lightning bolts coming closer and closer, and I wasn't about to let these gowns get wet. They were going to earn the homeless shelter thousands of dollars. With all those clothes in her closet, she wouldn't even know they were missing. How bad did she really want them with tags still attached? Just like the clothes she abandoned in Royal Palm Estates. How badly did she need those expensive clothes? She didn't. She just walked away.

How badly did she need a daughter? She didn't. She just walked away.

Rage and the onset of tears fueled my speed.

I also needed to get home before dad. I didn't want to explain the clothes if he saw them. My plan was to wheel the bike into the garage and leave the clothes until he went to sleep. Then go get them and hang them up.

Luckily, when I made it to our little home, just as cute in the dark with its white picket fence and window boxes, Dad's truck was not in the driveway. Whew. I managed to park the bike in the garage and whisk the clothes out of the basket and bolt into my room. I quickly hung them up to get any wrinkles out and placed the shoes on the floor of the closet.

Next, I ran into the shower and turned it as hot as I could stand it and jumped in, letting the scalding water pelt away the emotions of the day. The hot sting felt like relief, like it was burning the wrongness out of the stealing I had just done. I felt justified in so many ways. Justified for taking from her when she left me with nothing. Justified in taking from her when she was living in comfort, and I was left to suffer. Justified in taking from her when she left dad to die in the Everglades, while she jetted to New York and went shopping. No, I wasn't remorseful at all. But the hot steaming water helped. I don't know why, but it helped.

When my body got used to the heat, I reached down to the water spigot and turned it to freezing cold. The jolt to my body was electrifying. I stood there barely able to stand the cold, but I forced myself to. Finally, I got out and dried off, slipped on a t-shirt and shorts, and crawled into bed.

My phone rang. It was Leo. "Hey," I said trying to sound normal.

"Hey, your dad said you went with friends to watch the sunset and then coffee?" Leo sounded like he was surprised. And he had every right to sound this way because I never did those things. *He* was my best friend. *We* went everywhere together. Sometimes we went with Macy, Dexter, and the gang from school. But rarely. The kids from LWTHS were focused, driven kids. They studied and worked. Many of them had to help support their families. There wasn't much time for play.

I stared at the ring Leo had given me. The pretty gold ring with the aquamarine stone. Then, I grazed the charm bracelet and the dangling dolphin with my fingertips. I couldn't lie to Leo. I would never lie to Leo. I didn't even want to lie to dad, but I didn't want dad to worry about me. I felt the need to protect dad for some reason. Maybe because he was recovering from such an acute addiction that almost killed him. He was getting stronger every day, but there was still a vulnerability in his eyes. I needed him to stay focused on himself. Lying to him was protection.

Leo was different. He had an unshakable, quiet strength. It was one of many reasons I loved him. I knew I could tell him anything. I knew I had to tell him the truth. After all, staring at my ring, I promised.

So, I did. I told him everything that happened today. Everything. About going to Saks with Sharon and meeting Conrad McCormick. About how Brianna was with him. About the charity event. About Leo's dad giving me the address of Conrad McCormick's house and that Mom had run off with him. About lying to my dad. About riding my bike over there. About stealing. About hiding in the closest and hearing Conrad and Brianna. About going back and stealing again.

I told him everything. When I was finally finished, there was just silence on the phone.

His reaction was not what I expected.

Victoria

I couldn't sleep. I didn't want to get on that plane tomorrow. I didn't want to help McCormick with a fashion show. Fashion. Why did I let it rule my existence? Why were a group of people in charge of what other people were supposed to wear? As if wearing the right shoes made you more likable.   Suddenly, I felt like the whole fashion business was a scam. A scam on society. *Buy this new dress because last year's dress is out of style, and you don't want to be caught dead wearing something out of style now do you?* What a croc. And help Conrad? Why do I want to help Conrad with a fashion show?

In the beginning…………

   Once I had settled into my posh New York apartment, I set out to buy myself an entirely new wardrobe. After all, I had left everything behind. Shopping for new things gave me such a thrill. And I shopped for it all. New dresses. New shoes. New jewelry. Unlike Florida, the weather in New York dipped so cold that I finally bought chic winter clothes. Coats. Boots. Scarves. Gloves. I also redecorated the apartment, selecting a designer to help me pick out fabric for custom drapes, bedding, furniture, lamps, rugs, and accessories. I was finally getting to remodel without running out of money.

   It had been so long since I had total, unbridled reign over purchasing anything, that I went wild. For years, my paltry paycheck paid for utility bills and food.

And it was such a huge weight off my shoulders not to worry about bills anymore.

When thoughts of Vivian popped into my head, I convinced myself that her dad was taking care of her like he should be. That I was doing them a favor by forcing Collier to be responsible. That what I was doing was good for them. Tough love. That is what I was doing. Tough love.

Any remorse I felt for leaving her was shoved out of my mind by keeping myself extraordinarily busy. From the moment I got up each day, I went for workouts at the lavish gym in my building, spa treatments, hair appointments, nail appointments, shopping expeditions, lunches at chic bistros and dinners at fine restaurants with Conrad when he was in town. And Conrad expected me to always look fabulous. Keeping up with looking beautiful was a full-time job. A job that left little room for thoughts of regret.

And in the beginning, I had no regrets. I was going to tell Conrad the truth about Vivian and Collier one day soon. When the time was right, I would tell him everything. He would understand. One day soon. I would divorce Collier and explain that I loved Conrad. Vivian could come stay with me in New York every other weekend and during holidays and summers. Divorced kids had arrangements just like this. She would have fun shopping for anything she wanted. We could go to plays, museums, fine restaurants. Vivian would love it. I would tell Conrad all about her soon enough.

I promised myself I would. I really would.

Then one day over lunch, Conrad said, "Would you like to go to a designer fashion show? I'll introduce you to New York's top designers. Maybe you can show them some of your sketches."

I was so thrilled by this invitation that I raced back to my apartment after lunch. I sketched and sketched and sketched. My dream was coming true. I pictured myself with my own line of clothing with stunning models walking the runway in styles I created. Vogue Magazine featuring my new designer line. My own photo shoot wearing my unique creations.

The next day I was ready for the fashion show with my large leather portfolio of sketches when Conrad said, "Maybe today should just be a meet and greet. You can share your sketches later."

That seemed reasonable. I left the leather portfolio on the dining room table, and we were off to my first New York fashion show.

In the limo ride there, Conrad gave me instructions, "Now, many of these people know my wife, so I have a seat reserved for you a couple of rows behind me. You can follow me in, but don't act like you are my girlfriend. Act like we are business partners."

I felt a little weird about this conversation, but I guess he was right. I knew the bistros and restaurants we frequented were not ones he went to with his wife. I was his mistress after all. This is what I agreed to.

"Ok," is all I said, and I hung back as we entered the fashion show.

Conrad briefly pointed out where I was to sit and then left me alone. I watched as he went to shake hands with people he knew. He seemed to know a lot of models. Young models. And they fawned all over him, even giving him too friendly kisses and lingering hugs. He gushed over these 16-, 17-, and 18-year-old girls, loving all the attention they gave him and never once did he look at me.

I recognized two designers that walked over and began talking to him. He said he was going to introduce me, but he never even attempted to get my attention. I felt completely left out. Like he invited me but now had regrets about the invitation, so he ignored me.

As people took their seats, Conrad sat in the front row with a very young mystery girl next to him. He had his arm around her shoulders and frequently whispered something she thought was funny or interesting. My euphoric feeling from this morning was fading fast and confusion filled the voided space.

He wasn't introducing me to designers. He wasn't showing off my sketches. He wasn't even talking to me. He had promised. Why was he acting so distant?

When the show was over, I followed him to the limo and we both settled in. I was so hurt that I told him my feelings. I told him the truth. That I didn't like him talking and flirting with young girls. That it didn't seem right. That he was going to introduce me to designers. He had promised.

His reaction was not what I expected.

Chapter Thirteen

Vivian

"What the hell, Vivian?" Leo was furious.

His reaction completely caught me off guard. I thought he would understand. I guess I didn't give much thought to how he would react. He told me he loved me, so I just assumed he would understand. I have never heard him get upset about anything. Suddenly, my heart started to beat fast, and I sat up on my bed, ready to explain more. Ready to convince him that what I did was right. But he took command of the conversation and didn't let me speak.

"You have to take those things back. When I found out you took the money from Jewel last summer, I understood. You were hungry and needed to pay the bills on that house and you were young and didn't know what to do. I get that. Then you paid the money back and made it right. You can't just steal because you think there

113

is some kind of injustice. Stealing is not right, Vivian. Period."

Now I was getting mad. He was talking to me in such a self-righteous tone, and I hated it.

"How can you understand how I feel? You have the perfect family with normal parents!" I was trying not to yell, but my tone was angry and defensive. "You have no idea what it feels like to have your mother leave you," I stammered… "for a dress. Yes, that's right. She left because she would rather go shopping than be with me. Taking those dresses will teach her a lesson. No, I take that back. She won't even know they are missing because there were hundreds of dresses in her enormous closet! *Hundreds!* You should have seen it. Most of them still had tags on them!! I wanted to vomit!"

"Vivian, you can't just break into a house either. You shouldn't have even been there. You must take everything back and confront your mom. It is the right thing to do. My dad can go with you."

"Don't you dare tell your dad! If you tell your dad, I'm never speaking to you again!" I was crying now, knowing full well that was an idle threat.

"Hey, hey, hey, settle down, Vivian. I won't tell my dad, but you need to take everything back. I don't care how you do it. Just do it." He paused and my cries settled into silence. Silence that echoed in my tiny room.

I didn't say a word. I didn't know what to say next. I didn't know how to feel about what he was telling me to do. So, I said nothing and waited for him to say the next word.

Then, he broke the heavy quiet with a whisper. A whisper that pierced my soul.

"I cannot date a thief," Leo's firm, flat voice was hushed and hurt.

There was complete silence for what seemed like forever.

"Are you calling me a thief?" Anger laced my quivering voice.

Silence. Again. I carefully lowered my hand and stared at the glowing screen. With a deliberate tap, I hung up.

Dad poked his head in my room. I hadn't even realized he was back. "Everything Ok?"

"I'm fine." But I wasn't fine. I wasn't fine at all.

Victoria

In the beginning.......
Whap. The slap came so fast and so hard I was completely stunned. Instinctively, I put my hand to my

face to stop the sting. Suddenly afraid, I cowered and couldn't look at him. Was he going to hit me again?

"Don't act like that. I will do whatever I want whenever I want. Do you understand me?" His tone was visceral.

I nodded.

"I will introduce you to designers when I feel like it. And I will talk to whomever I want to talk to. You don't get to tell me who I can talk to. Is that clear?"

Another nod.

"I let you buy whatever you want, and you are to shut up and look pretty."

Anxiety gripped my chest, and I tried to breathe.

Silence filled the limo, and I dared to look up through my hair. Conrad was texting. I slowly straightened myself, smoothed my hair, and sat up taller, pretending everything was OK.

Conrad looked up from his phone directly into my eyes. "If you don't think you can handle this arrangement, leave. I'll put you on the next plane to Florida."

Stunned, I didn't know what to say but what slipped out without thinking was, "No. I'm sorry. It won't happen again. I'm fine." But I wasn't fine. I wasn't fine at all.

Chapter Fourteen

Vivian

When I woke up early Tuesday morning, I looked at my phone. 5:05 am. It was still dark, but I heard a bird chirping.

No call or text from Leo.

Dad wasn't up either. I was supposed to go to the work site with dad today and paint. I didn't want to see Leo. I pulled the covers back over my head. I would tell dad I was sick.   Another lie.

Two lies to dad in two days.

***

After dad left and the house was quiet, I got up. I opened my closet and stared at the dresses I took. Should I do what Leo said and take them back?

Maybe. Maybe he was right. But I also thought it was right to auction them off for charity. A charity that could save lives. Like dad's life had I not found him last

117

Christmas, laying in the scrub brush, wasting away to die. That image was resurrected, and anger filled my head again. How I had to curl up to him and give him sips of my water and crumbs from my muffin. How his eyes were glassy and delirious. How his anorexic body was melting into the Everglades.

No. I wasn't taking these dresses back. Leo didn't understand and if he couldn't understand me, then maybe we shouldn't be together. Tears stung my eyes, and I stared at the promise ring. I twisted it off my finger and set it on my dresser.

I wasn't going to take these dresses back to her.

But I *was* going to see if she showed back up at Conrad McCormick's.

I got dressed and grabbed my bike.

Victoria

In the beginning........

"You are going to love my private island," Conrad crooned with his arm around me. *"It is so remote and exquisite that it has become quite popular with a very discreet group of high-profile people."* Conrad bragged.

"In fact, I have invited several for the weekend. As my mistress, you must be very discreet as well. You cannot tell people who is on the island."

Fascinated, but a little uneasy about everything, I agreed and asked, "Who is coming?"

"I invited Prince James from Monaco, the president of Spain, Francisco Beladere, Senator Jason Peirre from California, Senator Jules Tanner from Massachusetts, and Judd Simons, a very wealthy businessman from North Carolina. There will also be several young lady guests. I expect you to be hospitable to everyone."

As the jet began its descent, my nerves began to grow. Powerful political people. Young girls. Secret island gatherings. This was not what I thought when I decided to run away with Conrad. What was I thinking, really? I knew nothing about him other than he was rich. That he made his own fortune and came from a poor family. That he was married and had teenagers. That was it. That is really all I knew. Why didn't I find out more before I made such a drastic move? What he offered me seemed like a quick out from my difficult circumstances. Running away with Conrad seemed like my ticket to freedom.... but I was realizing that ticket may have a very high price.

***

Dressed in an elegant white, off the shoulder gown with gold accessories, perfectly smooth blonde hair, and make-up that accentuated my features, I greeted Conrad's guests with style and grace. I looked at him, and he was staring at me with pride and desire.

I can do this, I kept telling myself.

The senators seemed pleasant enough, as did the prince, but the president of Spain was overly friendly and made me slightly uncomfortable. All was going well during the cocktail hour until four young girls presented themselves. I tried to keep my composure, but they were so young. As young as Vivian.... they had to be. I could tell they were trying to look older with the dresses they were wearing and make-up they had on, but there was no doubt these girls were barely over 18. One girl looked like one of the models Conrad ogled over at the fashion show. Certainly, Conrad wouldn't invite under aged girls to the island to meet up with these older men, would he?

That was against the law.

The model went straight to Conrad and hugged him. He forgot all about me and fixed his attention on her. The night went downhill from there. After far too much alcohol, Conrad and the model disappeared. The president of Spain wouldn't leave me alone, so I faked illness and retreated to an empty guest bedroom and locked the door.

The next morning there was pounding. I jumped and opened the door. Conrad raged into the room and shut the door and locked it. Smack! He slapped me so hard I fell to the floor. Then he kicked me several times in my stomach. I curled into a ball for protection with my hands over my head.

"Don't you ever act like that to a guest again! Do you hear me!! Francisco said you ignored his advances and ran away! You are to entertain my guests any way they want. You are not my wife. You are a mistress. You do as I tell you, and I told you to entertain my guests. You insulted him and now he is gone."

He gave me one more hard kick and exited the room, slamming the door.

***

Now, standing barefoot in the powdery white sand of this prison island, I asked myself, why didn't I leave when the abuse started? Why didn't I just go back to Florida and apologize to Collier and Vivian. Beg them to forgive me. Why? Was I worried they may reject me? Was I worried about getting a new job? Was I worried about dealing with a passed-out Collier? Was I worried about how I would get enough money to pay the bills? Yes. Yes. Yes. Yes.

Fear.

I was afraid to stay….and I was afraid to leave.

The jet was taking off in three hours. I slowly walked out to the water's edge, allowing the cool ocean waves to tickle my feet before the foam teased away. I walked further and further into the sea. My ankles. My knees. My chest. Then I went limp and melted into breathless, salty water.

Vivian

I rode back to McCormick's mansion again. I set the bike down right in the driveway. I wasn't going to break in this time. All I wanted was to see her face. To ask her why. That's it.

Bam Bam Bam…. *Bam Bam Bam*…. I stepped back and waited. And waited.

No answer. I tried several more times, but nothing.

I decided to walk around back and see if anyone was at the pool. The pool was deserted. I decided to cross the street and head to the beach.

I flipped off my sneakers and walked to the water's edge, looking out at the horizon, allowing the water to quench my hot feet and wondered.... *Where are you, mom?* I just need to see your face. Looking out to sea, I suddenly felt so homesick for her. When Leo's dad told me she was in town, that she was here, my desire to see her overwhelmed me. Now, I couldn't find her. Maybe he was mistaken. Maybe she was here, then left again.

I looked down at the sand and caught a glimpse of my ringless finger. Leo. He didn't understand the hurt inside me. He couldn't. I didn't want him to know this pain. Ever. I was such a mixture of emotions: anger, hatred, longing, sadness. There was an enormous gap in my heart that made me sick, and instead of it going away as time passed, it was growing.

Logic and Leo told me that giving back those gowns was the right thing to do, but I just couldn't do it. In some weird way, this kind of revenge lessened those angry emotions. If I could take something from her and use it to give to the needy, it somehow made my pain subside. Leo just didn't get it. Maybe he never would. Maybe being with me would be a lifetime of

123

complication for him. Like I am somehow damaged goods. I loved Leo so much. Maybe I needed to let him go, so he can live a quiet life with someone who comes from a normal family. Someone who doesn't have the urge to steal when enraged by injustice.

Who am I kidding, Leo let go of me. He saw the cracks. I can't give back those dresses. Those dresses are going to the homeless shelter. Period. Sorry Leo, but the need to ease my pain was uncontrollable.

I slipped back into my sneakers and walked back to my bike. The house was quiet and vacant. I decided to bike over to the airport. One last attempt to look for her. Maybe she was getting on that jet like she did last summer. I had to go see. Then I would give up. If she wanted to see me, she would have to find me.

***

It was about a twenty-minute bike ride to the airport and when I got there, I was hot and thirsty. I opened the terminal door and a gush of cool air hit my face. I looked around and spotted a water fountain.

As I was gulping down the icy water, I heard a voice.

"Vivian?" I turned and saw Blake, a student I knew pretty well from Lorenzo.

"Oh, hey Blake," I said politely, wiping the excess water off my chin with the back of my hand.

"What are you doing here?" he asked.

"Just killing time, watching planes," I lied.

"I love doing that too. When I was little, I used to beg my mom to drive here and park and let me just watch the jets take off and land. I could spend the whole day watching. I knew one day, I wanted to fly one of those babies. Then I fell in love with wanting to put them together."

I knew Blake was in the aviation mechanics program at Lorenzo. We watched several jets land and take off. We talked about planes and school and our futures. It was nice to just talk to someone not involved in my life. While we were hanging out, I studied to see if my mom was anywhere in sight. Several people boarded and got off planes, but no mom anywhere.

"Are you working today?"

"Yea, I'm on a break now."

We walked over to the glass wall and just looked at all the private jets lined up on the runway.

"Hey, do you think you could find out if a particular private plane took off recently?"

"I don't know. Let's go ask." We walked over to the ticket counter.

"I think my mom left recently on Mr. McCormick's plane," I said to an older lady at the check-in counter, acting like this was an average request from a rich Portofino kid.

"I'm really not supposed to do this, but let's see," She hesitated while looking at me, then Blake. "Well, since Blake works here, I suppose you must be harmless." She started scrutinizing her logbook. "Yes, Mr. McCormick's jet took off yesterday. Victoria James. Is she your mom? She was on the plane."

My heart sank. "Where did she go?"

"It looks like a private island in the Bahamas."

"Thanks."

I said goodbye to Blake, quickly, so he wouldn't see my anger and sped away on my bike.

I am never giving back those dresses. I thought as I peddled faster and faster. And I'm never looking for her again.

She is dead to me.

Chapter Fifteen

Vivan

After several unanswered texts from Leo, I finally responded to his last plea to meet. It was late and dad was asleep, but I agreed to meet him in the driveway. As painful as this was going to be, I knew what I had to do.

Phone in my pocket along with a small navy velvet box, I walked out to wait, but didn't have to because he was already sprinting down the street. His muscular body effortlessly floating in air. For a moment, physical excitement flooded my veins. I tried to push away those emotions, but when he approached, he swept me into his arms with kind forcefulness and kissed me so passionately, I didn't have time to resist. Then my body refused to listen to my head and for a few hot minutes, I released my emotions and kissed him back, with uncontrollable power.

"I love you so much, Vivian, I really do," he breathed between kisses.

I didn't respond. I loved him, too, without question, but knew that I had to let go. I couldn't put him through my grief and pain. I forcefully pushed him back, unlocking our kiss.

"I didn't take those dresses back and I'm not going to," I said, looking down at the paved driveway. I didn't want to see his reaction. Then, forcing myself to be brave, I looked up at his face, and there I saw it. What I didn't want to see. Disappointment. Hurt. He thought I would come to my senses and do the right thing. He thought I would give the dresses back. For him. For us. But I didn't. I couldn't. And I would not let him compromise his values to be with a thief. Leo was right. Even if I justified my actions in my own mind, that is really what I was, a thief. I knew what I had to do.

I reached into my pocket and pulled out a tiny box and when he saw what I was doing, tears formed in his amazingly beautiful blue eyes, and it looked like I was staring into the sea. The fact that I was causing this pain to him was almost unbearable.

"You can't be with a person like me. I am damaged. My emotions are too raw and need healing. I just can't be in a relationship with someone as wonderful as you. You deserve so much more. You deserve a person without all my baggage. And I don't know how long it is going to take me to heal. My mom is probably never coming back, by her own choice, and that is something I have to live with every day. And you can't understand that hurt. It is like a death—only worse—because not only do I never get to see her again, but I have to live with the fact that she rejected me. That she didn't love me enough to stay. And I just don't think I will ever be whole because of it. Ever."

Lightning lit the sky, followed by a boom of thunder, but we didn't budge. I had stepped back to resist the electric passion we shared, and we were now standing a few feet apart. The sky let out spits of rain that slowly gained power. "And I love you too much to put you through a life with a flawed person. Because you are not flawed—at all. You are amazing and deserve amazing." I was crying uncontrollably now.

He just stood there, stunned, crying too. I continued, "You said you couldn't be with a thief. That if I didn't give back those dresses, you couldn't be with me." He tried to interrupt, but I wouldn't let him. "And you are right. You shouldn't be with a thief. And don't try to say you could, because eventually you would resent me for it. Because it goes against your principles and you are completely right, but you will NEVER understand my pain. NEVER! And I don't want you to understand it. Taking those dresses and giving them to charity eases my pain. It just does. And I can't help it. And I'm going to do it." Now my tears were mixed with a forceful, angry voice.

I stretched out my arm and opened my balled-up fist holding the box with the promise ring in it. He refused to take it. He didn't even lift an arm. He just stared into my eyes, pleading. I took two steps forward and grabbed his wrist to force him to take the box, but his fist was clenched. It was pouring now, and we were drenched.

I carefully bent down and placed the box on the driveway and walked back into my house, passing the window boxes where little orange and yellow sunshines were getting pummeled with large, wet water pellets.

Victoria

I floated freely, fearlessly, allowing the swell to lift and lower my body as I stared at the sky. What if I decided to go back to Portofino? Explain everything to Vivian and Collier. Ask them to forgive me. Plead with them. Would they forgive? Could they forget? Never. How could they forget what I did? The deplorable thing I did. Leaving them. Leaving them for an easier life......easier life? Ha! What a fool I have been.

Collier might understand. He might forgive me.
But Vivian? She would never understand.

Chapter Sixteen

Vivian

"Vivian, these dresses are amazing! Why haven't you brought these to me before? And the shoes," Sharon was gaping in awe. "We will make thousands for the charity."

"I was saving them for sentimental reasons. You know in case mom returned, but I would rather the money go to charity." Little lies for a lovely cause.

"Are you sure?"

"I'm positive."

"Arnie said we can have only six outfits up for auction. That is three a piece. Today let's pick everything out and tomorrow we will practice walking the catwalk," Sharon giggled with delight.

I had gotten so good at separating my emotions over the last few years from painful home life to fake middle school life, that my feelings for Leo were shoved away for now. In fact, I buried them so deep into an unseen-by-the-naked-eye crack in my brain that only a roach could find and slip through.

Today, was about dad and our charity and Sharon and her opportunity to let her business shine in the community.

As we tried on clothes, we laughed and had fun figuring out the best ensembles. Sharon fit perfectly into two of mom's more mature styled dresses and shoes. I fit into the strapless pink one that was clearly too young for mom, but she probably wanted to look younger by wearing it. We each picked out other outfits that were stunning and agreed that Saks and McCormick's, along with Portofino's other fine retailers, would be shocked at our sophisticated inventory.

After we finished with our final fittings, Sharon said, "Vivian, there is a special guest speaker in town about a charity I have recently gotten involved in, and the church is having a potluck barbeque at Lowery Park to listen to her speak. I want you to come with me. It is just for women and teenage girls. I think you would like it because my charity is teaming up with the Portofino Homeless Shelter for this cause."

"Yes, I would like that very much," I said, thinking this would be a great diversion from my emotions and a way to avoid Leo if he tried to see me tonight. "What is the charity?"

"It is called Harmony House. It's a place for women and teens to go who are rescued from the sex trafficking trade."

.   "Oh," I was momentarily uncomfortable but regained my maturity. "What time?"

"6:00. Could you call your dad? Then we can just go from here after we close the shop at 5:00. I need to stop and get something to take for the potluck, and we can help set up."

"Sure, dad won't mind," I paused, then said, "Sharon, is sex trafficking that big of a problem?"

"Honey, you have no idea how bad it is. It is very hard to research the numbers, but studies are showing that there are 15,000 to 50,000 women and children just in the United States and as many as 600,000 - 800,000 across international borders each year. It is terrible."

Victoria

Instead of floating out to sea, my body washed ashore at 5:00.

Chapter Seventeen

Vivian

When we got to Lowery Park, the traffic was jammed and there wasn't a parking spot. "Wow, look at all the people. I heard this speaker was good, and I'm thrilled so many will hear about this cause. Hopefully, awareness will bring change," Sharon said. "Vivian, there are so many young girls, like you, being lured into this dark world. They don't even know what is happening to them until it is too late, and then they are prisoners."

We found a parking place a block away, and Sharon grabbed the giant fruit tray from the backseat. I loved Sharon. She had become my surrogate mom this last year, and I was happy she was in my life. We set the tray on a long table and helped other ladies I recognized from church organize plates, napkins, and the assortment of food and drinks.

The minister's wife led everyone in a prayer followed by an hour of eating and making small talk with people. Then, we settled into our lawn chairs for a bible reading and introduction of the cause and the guest speaker.

"Thank you all for coming out to this gorgeous sunset in beautiful Portofino, Florida. It is hard to imagine looking around at all the luxury and serenity that this seemingly simple, quiet town could be a place where teens are being forced into prostitution. But that is exactly what is happening. You have heard about sex trafficking, and I'm sure you think it is only in some distant seedy city far from here, but that is not the case. Sex trafficking is also right here in your backyard.

Harmony House is a Christian organization that's main purpose is to find these women and young teens and rescue them. Did you know that when a teen runs away, it takes only 48 hours before they are approached by a sex trafficker? They are often lured in with the promise of money, fancy clothes, and basic needs like food and shelter. These very young girls have no idea of the nefarious intentions of their predators. We have local missionaries that drive the streets looking for girls and boys who have run away. We have teamed up with local police to assist so that these teens trust us. Once we suspect a teen has run away, we call the police and within minutes, they are there to help. Harmony House also has a hotline for girls to call who are already in trouble and again, we call police to rescue them from their situation and bring them to Harmony House.

Most of the time, these girls are not kidnapped outright like you might see in a movie but lured with gifts and promises of wealth and comfort. Once they agree to go with the predator, they are trapped, often abused, both physically and mentally, into thinking they are worthless and can't escape.

People also have misconceptions about who is doing the luring and trafficking. We have found that there is no economic or social status unaffected by this problem. Wealthy communities like Portofino have people with power and money who commit these sex crimes. In fact, they are trusted because they seem legitimate with their fancy clothes, cars, homes and connections with local businesses and institutions.

These predators prey on vulnerable teens and women. People who are going through pain and difficulty. Girls from broken homes and abusive families are in particular danger." The speaker was going on with statistics that were alarming. When she finally came to her conclusion, she said, "We are asking for donations today to help with the recovery process at Harmony House. Women and teens get food, shelter and counseling. We also have educators who teach them skills, so they can survive on their own. We don't want you to feel pressured to give. Just being here tonight and becoming aware that this is a problem in your own community is most important. Maybe instead of money, you may want to volunteer at Harmony House. Maybe you have some special skills and talents you can share or just volunteer to cook and counsel with words of hope."

When the speaker was finished, the wealthy women of Portofino were writing checks and giving them to the ushers who were standing in the back with offering plates. Watching Sharon thank the people who came, with such genuine appreciation, made me wish my mom was more like her. I thought she once was, when I was little, but maybe I was wrong. Maybe I just didn't see Mom's obsession with personal wealth, but I remember her being kind like Sharon. People liked my mom. I liked my mom when I was little. No, I *loved* my mom. I remember she used to tease me that when I first learned to talk, I grabbed her face with my tiny hands and said, 'you are my best friend.' She told everyone that story. She loved me. A lot. Back then. Sharon reminded me of the old mom. The one I knew from childhood. The one I longed for. The one I had to forget.

Victoria

I felt my body being lifted. Where was it going?
Heaven? Hell? I heard horns….traffic?

Chapter Eighteen

Vivian

It was Thursday, and Sharon and I put on fun, happy music to practice modeling on the catwalk. We playfully exaggerated our poses and turns, laughing and laughing until tears formed. It was hard to believe I could be laughing, genuinely laughing, with the realization my mom rejected my existence and my breakup with Leo was still warm, but I was. And the laughter was purging the pain at precisely the right moment.

Leo had not left any message, and I was glad. I had exterminated those emotions for now and would deal with them later. When I was alone.

Dressed in our glamourous gowns, Sharon and I were about to change into normal clothes when the front door violently flew open, and Sarah burst through in a wild panic. She wasn't with her posse, Brianna and Bella, and looked like she was being chased, eyes wild and freaking out.

"Vivian! You need to help me!" Sarah shouted, breathing so hard I could barely understand her.

"What is it?" I asked, frozen and bewildered.

"It's Brianna and Bella. They told their parents that they were spending the night with me. But they were actually going to Mr. McCormick's house to practice modeling for the fashion show. I thought the whole thing was creepy and weird and told them I didn't want to go. They told me he wasn't going to let anyone model unless he saw that they were good enough. He said he didn't want his store to be embarrassed. I told them I didn't want to do it. So, I guess they told their parents they were staying with me. Anyway," she was catching her breath and spewing the story as fast as she could. "Brianna called me this morning and told me Mr. McCormick put something in their drinks last night and they passed out. Brianna is awake, but she won't leave Bella. Bella is still passed out, but she said she is breathing and OK. She just won't budge. Brianna said they are on Mr. McCormick's yacht parked at the dock. I need your help. Quick!"

Sharon took command and said, "Why did you come to us? Why didn't you tell your parents and call the police?" Sharon was grabbing her purse and keys and she locked the front door after we rushed to follow her out. "And how did you get here?"

141

"I had my mom drop me off at the mall and told her I was meeting Brianna and Bella. Then I ran all the way here." Sarah looked at Sharon when we were opening car doors and then me, "Brianna begged me not to call the police and she told me to get you, Vivian......" Sarah paused and Sharon and I froze for a second to listen when she added, "Brianna said she saw your mom in the house. Brianna's voice was shaking so badly, and she was whispering so I hardly heard her, but I think she said your mom is in trouble."

We all exchanged a worried, but powerful look, a look of pure strength and bravado, and jumped into Sharon's car, with Sarah in the back seat and Sharon and me in the front.

"Vivian, get Leo's dad on the phone. Now! Sarah, do you know the address?" Sharon shouted as we squealed away from the curb.

"No," she said.

"I do," I commanded. "Take a left at the light."

Sharon gave me a quick, quizzical look, but didn't ask how I knew the address. She just drove as fast as she could.

Victoria

"Where am I?" I had come to and could see I was on Conrad's jet. Maxwell was sitting across from me.

"You need to get it together. Now. I showered you, blew your hair dry and managed to dress you. How…I have no idea, but I have your make up bag and you need to do the rest. You have about 30 more minutes. Then I'm taking you to Mr. McCormick's. Remember, you are helping with the fashion show on Friday. Have you taken any drugs? You should never swim after taking drugs. I found you nearly dead on the shore."

I had taken something before I went to sea. Sleeping pills. Double the dose. But now I was waking up. The last thing I remembered was floating on the sea and then hitting the shore with a vague recollection of someone lifting me. Maxwell said nothing about this. He said nothing about why or what's going on or are you OK. He would do practically anything for the man who probably paid him plenty. Why would he care about me? The only reason he rescued me from the beach was to deliver me to Conrad.

I took the make-up bag and managed to steady myself to the bathroom. After several minutes, I returned to my seat. Maxwell gave me a hard look over and said, "Better."

Tucked in the magazine rack, I saw my sketch pad. I grabbed it and opened the pages, looking at the sketches. They weren't bad.... but they weren't great either. I closed it and shoved it in my bag. I didn't want to leave anything of mine here. I was never going to get on this plane again. After this fashion show, I was going to leave. In fact, as my head got clearer, I had an idea to make a scene at the fashion show in front of others. That way he would have to let me go.... or people would get suspicious. Maybe my failed attempt to drift to sea was a sign that I needed to try to ask Vivian and Collier for forgiveness. I would find them and ask. What could it hurt? If they said no, I would find one of those shelters and figure my life out. Start over. Maybe in time Vivian would forgive me.

"Can I have some tea?" I asked Maxwell. Having a plan made me a bit more confident.

***

Once we got to McCormick's Portofino mansion, it was getting dark, and when I entered the foyer, I heard laughter from the kitchen. Not in the mood to talk to Conrad or any of his guests, I slipped into the bedroom, unseen.

Maxwell must have announced my arrival to Conrad because a few minutes later he burst through the door. "I'm entertaining the models for the fashion show. I promised them a sunset cruise around the bay. I asked the girls to spend the night, so you can help them get ready for the show tomorrow."

This was so strange. I couldn't stand it anymore. "Who is it?" Worried it was Brianna or any girl far too young to be here.

Slap! He whacked me across the face. "I don't answer to you. And I would beat the shit out of you right now for your tone if I didn't need that pretty face for the next two days. But I'm going to warn you." He sneered, "If you try any funny business, after the show, I will personally make you my punching bag. I could use a good workout."

He slammed the door on the way out.

My mind raced. I wanted to leave right then, but I knew it was Vivian's friends out there. I had to do something. Call the police? On what grounds? He was touring some girls on his boat. He had so much money, the police would laugh at me and then what? Get beat up.

I decided to walk out to the kitchen and stay close to the girls to protect them. He couldn't do anything to them if I was there watching. I don't think.

145

Nervous, but determined now, I opened the door. But I was too late. The boat was pulling away from the dock. I ran out by the pool and down the catwalk that led to the dock. I saw Brianna with a drink in her hand and someone else I couldn't make out.

I fidgeted for about an hour in the kitchen, waiting for them to return. It was dark now. Finally, the boat banked at the dock and Conrad opened the sliders and saw me in the kitchen.

"Where are your models?" I asked, trying to sound matter a fact.

"On the boat. They are practicing a bit more for me," and he gave an arrogant laugh. I could tell he had been drinking.

"I'm going to come join you guys," I grabbed my glass of water and walked his way.

Conrad grabbed my wrist harshly, and I was suddenly reminded of the first dinner I had with him over a year ago, when he grabbed my wrist like this. I justified his actions by saying he was strong, confident, knew what he wanted in life. Ha! I should have run. I should never have gone out with him again. Big mistake. But now, I was going to do something good. Something to make up for my grave error in judgement.

"No, you are not. You will spoil the fun. That is what you are," his voice was slightly slurred. "a fun spoiler. Why did I ever like you? You are pretty, but that is it. I thought you liked to drink and have a good time when I met you. You were different then. Now, you don't like to party and get wild. Fun killer. That's what you are."

"No, I'll come have some fun," I tried to sound upbeat, but he was on to me.

"What are you drinking?" He sniffed my drink. "Water? You are drinking water? You lying bitch! You don't want to have fun. You want to stop the fun."

I squared my shoulders and mustered up as much confidence as I could. I don't know how I let him control me all year. But I knew I wasn't going to let him take advantage of those girls. I had to do something.

"I saw Brianna on that boat. She is 15 years old. You can't let 15-year-olds spend the night on your boat. You are 60 years old. That is against the law! And disgusting!" As if this wasn't enough to bring his rage to a boil, I added the nail in my own coffin. "If you don't tell those girls to go home now, I'm calling the police."

He lunged for me, grabbing my neck in his drunken mania. Eyes bulging, face contorted and red, his grip fueled with fury clamped down like an iron vice constricting my airways. Unable to breathe, I tried choking out words to stop but couldn't. I felt my body deflating and thought, this is the end of me. I'm going to

die in Conrad's kitchen. I will never see Vivian or Collier
again. I deserve this. I relinquished any fight I had in
me.   And when I did, he let go. I began to stumble
backwards, gasping for air, and that is when I saw the fist
coming right for my head. Then, I hit the floor. My eyes
opened and my cheek was cold against the marble. Kicks
kept coming over and over. Profane, degrading slurs, one
after the other as he kicked and beat me. And kicked and
beat me in a drunken rage.

Until there was nothing but darkness.

Chapter Nineteen

Vivian and Victoria

Leo's dad and his partner pulled up to the house at the same time as we did.

"We have reinforcements coming. You all stay here," Mr. Lamont's baritone voice boomed authority.

I repeated everything Sarah had said to me, including the girls were on the boat and mom was in trouble. Without knocking, Mr. Lamont tried the front door, but it was locked. He and another officer hustled around to the back as two more police cars showed up and four more officers quickly got out.

I heard Mr. Lamont radio for assistance and two of the four policemen hurried to the back of the McCormick mansion. Within a few seconds I heard a siren. And it was getting louder. An officer opened the front door, coming out from inside.

As soon as the paramedics got there, they raced in. The first to come out was Bella, limp in a medic's

149

arms with Brianna being carried like a little kid by an officer. She was crying.

"Oh No!" said Sarah.

Then on a stretcher, Mom lay lifeless as two giant medics carried her out through the large wooden front door.

I lunged towards the stretcher, not caring that the police were yelling to stay back. I hadn't seen her in over a year and every built-up bitter feeling flew away, forgotten.

I screamed, "Mooooom!!!!!"

An officer grabbed me and said, "Calm down. Your mom is OK. But she is seriously injured. Let the paramedics get her to the hospital as soon as they can."

Sarah said, "What about Bella?"

"She will be OK. They need to give both girls exams, but physically, they are going to be fine."

"Mr. McCormick is passed out drunk. Officers are hand cuffing him to take him to the station," said the officer.

We followed the ambulance to the hospital, and I called dad who met us there. We all paced nervously in the waiting room, Sharon, Sarah, Dad and me.

Finally, a doctor emerged.

"Mr. James," Dad stepped closer. "Your wife suffered a bad concussion, three broken ribs, and several bruises. She is currently in a coma, and we are not sure when or if she will come out of it at this point."

Dad teared up and asked, "Can we see her?" The doctor led the way as Dad and I followed.

Mom's head was bandaged, and her eyes were black and blue. She looked so weak. So fragile. So damaged. It was impossible not to feel sorry for her.

Dad rushed to her side with tears streaming down his face and uttered, "Sorry, Vicki. I am so so sorry." He began sobbing.

Every hateful thought I had in the last year dissipated when I saw her like this, when I heard Dad's tearful, remorseful words. Was it possible she hadn't been living the luxury life I imagined? What kind of sick person does this to another human?

Not really knowing what to do and trying to make myself useful, I grabbed a chair for dad, and he pulled it up close to mom's bed and held her hand gently. He laid his head on the embrace and began to cry harder. I felt awkward suddenly. Like I was an intruder to their reunion. I walked over to dad and rubbed his back.

"Dad, I'm going to go home with Sharon and change clothes," I whispered, suddenly aware of how grossly overdressed I appeared in my elaborate pink puffy ball gown.

He snuffled back his emotions momentarily and whispered back, "Bring me an overnight bag with a change of clothes and toothbrush and stuff. I'm not leaving her side. I want to be here when she wakes."

When I returned to the waiting room, Sharon told me that Sarah's mom had come to get her. As the two of us were leaving the hospital, we bumped into Leo's dad.

"How are Brianna and Bella?" I asked.

"They are going to be fine. They got lucky. They had not been violated by Mr. McCormick. He passed out drunk before any harm could be done. Brianna did tell me one thing I think you should know, Vivian. She said that the last thing she remembered before she blacked out was that Mr. McCormick told the girls that your mom was going to stop 'the fun' and that 'nobody stops him from doing what he wants,' and that 'she got what she deserved for being a fun killer.' Both girls passed out from the drug he slipped into their drinks, and when Brianna came to in the morning, she remembered what he said and rushed up and found your mom on the floor and called Sarah," he paused. "Your mom was going to stop the abuse of the girls, probably knowing the consequences she faced. I just thought you should know that."

On the slow, quiet ride back to Sharon's Riches, my head was so full of thoughts that it felt about to burst.

What had happened to mom over the last year? How could she have fallen for a guy like that? Why didn't she just come home? Was she going to survive this? Tears escaped my eyes and fell into my lap as I pressed my forehead against the car window.

***

We cancelled our participation in Arnie's fashion show. Sharon told me we would have our own event one day soon and donate the proceeds. Fashion shows were the last thing on my mind. All I wanted right now was for my mom to come out of her coma.

***

One week had passed and dad and I spent every night in the hospital. The nurses pulled in two recliner chairs, and we slept in them, never leaving her side except to take turns using the restroom or getting some food in the cafeteria—although neither of us had much of an appetite.

One day, when I was going to get a snack, I froze as I came face to face with Leo and his dad. Leo's compassionate countenance instinctively sensed my tension, and he gently walked over and hugged me tight. I couldn't resist his embrace. In fact, I melted into him as if he was the oxygen I needed to survive. Taking a deep breath, then exhaling slowly, tears sprung involuntarily, releasing all the emotion I had been bottling up this past week. After clinging together for a few minutes, Mr. Lamont spoke, breaking our quiet reunion, and I let go, stepping back from Leo.

"I need to talk to you, Vivian. It's about Mr. McCormick. And you are not going to like it. Have a seat." Mr. Lamont's quiet, baritone voice continued as we all found some seats in the corner of the waiting room. "Conrad McCormick was released this morning."

"WHAT?!" I almost screamed.

"Shhhh Vivian. I know this is upsetting. It is upsetting to me, too. He must have friends in very high places because his attorney got his sentence reduced to a misdemeanor domestic violence charge. All he has to do is some community service. The department is furious. We have decided to launch our own investigation into this creep. See if he has abused other women and girls. Conrad McCormick hasn't seen the last of me."

I couldn't believe what I was hearing. I thought he would go to jail. He almost killed my mother and if she doesn't survive, he will have killed her! How could anyone let him out?

Fury flooded my body. There was no way that I was going to back down from that piece of trash. I was going to crawl all over that garbage dump of a human. I wanted to make him suffer. Suffer for luring my mom away from me. Suffer for hurting her. Suffer for preying on young girls –ick. You are an icky, creepy, scumbag, and I am coming after you myself. Watch out waste of a person, Roach Girl is about to infest your world.

Leo must have seen the madness emanating from my every pore because he said, "Vivian, do not get any ideas. Let my dad and the police handle this. This guy sounds like bad news. You can't go anywhere near him. He is dangerous."

Leo's dad looked at Leo and then me, suddenly realizing the look on my face that worried Leo. "Leo is right, Vivian. You cannot go anywhere near that house. In fact, you need to stay out of sight for a while. Until we can get this guy behind bars. I'm guessing there are girls out there with a story to tell about Conrad McCormick. Until then, don't take matters into your hands. Are you listening, Vivian."

"I'm listening," I said.

But I didn't promise a thing. The urge for revenge pulsed inside me. I felt like I did when I stole from the unscrupulous to give to the needy. Stealing felt like revenge, and revenge felt so satisfying. I needed revenge on Mr. McCormick. And I didn't know if I could contain myself.

Chapter Twenty

Vivian

On day eight, Mom's hand made a slight movement. Dad sprang to her side and brushed his fingers lightly with hers. Again, her fingers moved as if trying to find Dad's. I rushed out to get the nurse, who contacted the doctor, and within minutes a team of people were checking her vital signs.

Not much more happened that day, but on the next day, she moved her head and barely opened her eyes a few times.

And that is how she slowly began to regain consciousness.

A little at a time.

Filled with hope that she was recovering, my mind was constantly at odds with my emotions. I was happy she was getting better each day, confused about why she would leave us for someone like Mr.

McCormick, and angry about what McCormick did to mom and didn't have to pay a price.

In fact, that last emotion filled me with constant waves of rage that would ebb and flow like the tides of the ocean. When I was little, mom and dad would take me to the beach a lot. If we went early in the morning, the Gulf of Mexico was peaceful and calm, almost like turquoise glass, barely making a ripple as it gently met the sand. But if we went late in the afternoon, the waves were forceful and strong, crashing violently on the shore, sometimes too much, making the undertow deadly. That is how my emotions were, sometimes calm and peaceful, sometimes raging with strength bordering on dangerous.

Doctors warned us that mom's future was still uncertain. They told us that head injuries and severe strangling can cause a range of long-term effects like mobility, speech, and memory problems. Only time would tell if mom would walk, talk, and think like before.

Dad insisted I sleep at home and come to the hospital only during the day. Sharon agreed to stay with me. On the first night home, I fell asleep after supper around 7:00 and slept like I hadn't had any rest in ten years. My body took over and pulled me into such a deep slumber, I sunk into a vivid nightmare, one so real and so frightening. My body had mutated into a frightening, gigantic roach and while I could fly, it wasn't exhilarating, it was terrifying and nauseating. The airborne movements were erratic and jerky, like I didn't know which way to turn and flee. So, my light, weightless, transparent, copper wings darted me around in staccato indecisiveness, making my body and brain throb and thunder. *Where do I go for food? Where do I go for shelter and safety? Where can I hide from the monster? Was I at Royal Palm Estates with no food or water? Was I in a mansion by the sea?*

I woke, dripping with sweat. My head darted around the dark room trying to recall where I was. My room. Not Royal Palm Estates. Not McCormick's mansion. Not starving. Not fighting the monster. Not stealing his jewels. My heart settled slowly as did my breathing.

It was just a dangerous dream. But as I gained consciousness, I liked the nightmare. In fact, the nightmare wasn't a nightmare at all. It was a sign. A sign that if McCormick didn't have to pay a price for almost killing my mom, I knew someone who would make him pay—someone I knew very well. Someone who wasn't afraid of anything or anyone. Someone who survived when worlds crumbled.

Roach Girl.

Victoria

Every time I opened my eyes, I saw him. Collier. Was it really him? Was he really sitting beside me holding my hand? I tried so hard to keep them open because when I closed them, I went to a dark, dark place. Conrad. The beating. The abuse. The fear. What happened to the girls on the boat? Where is Conrad? Could he hurt me again? Could he hurt young girls? Could he hurt Vivian? Where was he?

Every time I opened my eyes, I tried to speak, but nothing came out. Collier would utter, "Shhhh. Honey, you need to rest and gain strength. There will be time to talk." I tried to smile at him to let him know I was thankful he was there, but my face hurt so badly.

Every time I closed my eyes, my anxiety heightened. My fear deepened. My dark world took over. I knew Conrad was out there. Somewhere. That monster needs to be stopped.

Chapter Twenty-one

Vivian

I crept around our little house in the dark, hoping not to disturb Sharon. I slipped on my bathing suit, shorts, and sneakers, and secured my large backpack around my shoulders. The sun would be up soon, and I would already be gone. I scribbled a note and left it on the table.

An early morning swim in the calm waters of the Gulf is exactly what I needed, and I knew exactly where I wanted to take that swim. I peddled, in the now gray morning sky, towards Olde Portofino.

My nightmare might be over, but my mission had just begun.

Victoria

I watched Collier creep around the hospital room thinking I was asleep and hoping not to disturb me. My head felt heavy and dull. My eyes felt heavy and sore. My body felt heavy and useless. When Collier saw me trying to keep my eyes open, he smiled and rushed back to my bedside.

"Do you feel stronger?" he asked.

I couldn't nod my head or lift my hand or utter a word. When I tried to speak, I sounded like a sick whale. Tears wet my face.

"Shhh. Don't. Not now. We both have a lot of things to explain and apologize for. I feel so responsible for so much, but I want to move forward. When the doctors say it is OK, I want you to come home. I will take complete care of you. I owe you that and more. And once you have completely recovered, we will talk," Collier hesitated before going on. "Do you want to come home?" He suddenly sounded vulnerable.

Tears streamed faster, and I thought I was in a dream. I couldn't even choke out my answer. With all my strength, I managed a slight nod. How could he want me back after I left him for another man? How could he say he felt responsible? This was all my fault. I deserved

exactly what I got. I deserved to be beaten. I shouldn't
even be alive. I deserved death.

Chapter Twenty-two

Vivian

Although the McCormick mansion wasn't on the beach, it was directly across the street from it. Many of the world's wealthiest families preferred the grand homes on the bay so they could park their enormous yachts right in their backyards and slip out to sea easily.

I rode my bike casually past the mansion. It was dead quiet and appeared vacant. I whisked back quickly, up the driveway and hid my bike in the same spot behind a hedge. I had no intention of knocking on the door to see if he was home. I had become a pro at moving around stealthily, jumping gates with such agility, and slinking from spot to spot undetected, that I should become a spy.

Instead, I had become a thief. A thief who found relief from her pain by stealing from the rich to give to the poor. If McCormick could get away with almost murdering a person, almost raping a person, then I could get away with a simple theft. In fact, the idea of taking from him electrified me in a way I couldn't explain. No one could understand how this forbidden vice didn't seem unlawful when it was driven by a force to make things right. In fact, it felt so right. Like the rightest thing I had ever done in my life.

Leo would disagree. Leo would tell me that two wrongs do not make a right. Leo would tell me he couldn't date me anymore if I continued to steal. And as much as I loved Leo, I was consumed by this need to even the playing field. This need for revenge. This need to take something from that monster who hurt my mom, who intended to hurt Brianna and Bella, who probably hurt others.

I tried every sliding door with blinking speed. All locked.

Unsure what to do next and not wanting to draw attention to myself, I quickly hopped on my bike and ambled across the street to the beach. I laid my bike down in the sand as the sun was coming up from the Everglades, casting a clear blue sky over the Gulf. Even though it was early morning, the summer air was sticky, and the water melted away the heat.

Swimming was still my favorite thing to do, so I just started gliding through the slick, salty water. I swam and swam and swam until I knew I should turn around and swim back. I reached the spot with my bike and flopped my tired body on the sand.

How was I going to get into the McCormick mansion? Think.

I rinsed off my sandy body at the beach shower next to the street and noticed a Mandy Maids van in McCormick's driveway. My back stiffened with excitement. Opportunity knocks. Acting casual, I rode my bike past his driveway, just out of view, and hid it in the neighbor's tall hedge. Most of these millionaires were gone this time of year and the neighbor's house looked just as vacant as McCormick's.

Wearing my expensive bathing suit, cut off shorts and blonde hair loose and air drying, I looked like a typical rich Portofino kid and if I got caught, that is how I would act—a bored, privileged teen looking for a friend. I ponged from bush to bush until I was right near the front door and waited for the right moment.

I didn't have to wait long. A housekeeper came out to get supplies and left the door cracked open. I slipped in before she turned around.

Knowing the main floor layout, I crept into the closet where I hid from Mr. McCormick and Brianna just days ago, carefully pulling out rubber gloves I had in my pocket, closing the door shut, and maneuvering behind coats to a corner where I was completely hidden. I waited. As I stood still in the dark, I forced myself to breathe silently. My nose barely touched the leather coat keeping me hidden. Carefully inhaling the distinct smell of animal hide, I closed my eyes, and my mind began to wander. What are you doing here, Vivian? What is stealing from this man going to do? He can just buy something new—if he even realizes anything is missing. What if McCormick catches you? Look what he did to mom? To Brianna and Bella? What are you thinking? Panic gripped my chest, and I found myself struggling to breathe quietly. Eyes still closed, I deeply and silently inhaled and exhaled, slowing down the panic.

Then I felt a tickle on my leg. Opening my eyes, I glanced down to see a tag hanging by a string attached to the inside of the sleeve of the leather coat. I lifted the tag to an inch in front of my face and read $18,300! What?!? Panic and regret were instantly replaced with vengeance and fury. Anxiously, I waited for the front wooden door to shut tight behind the last housekeeper. Silence filled the air beyond the closet door, so I finally emerged. I went straight for the main bedroom closet. The one where I stole Mom's dresses. I didn't waste time looking at Mom's clothes, nor did I hesitate. Immediately, I began opening drawers and fumbling through socks and underwear, careful to put everything back precisely.

I opened the last bottom drawer and thought this was going to be a bust when, bingo! Just what I was looking for. Something of value. Something of his. Something I could steal. Something I could pawn. Not one, but two exquisite Rolex watches.

A trip to see Roy at the Priceless Pawn was long overdue.

But first, I had to go home.

Victoria

I heard a noise. Harnessing as much effort as I could manage, I opened my eyes to see who had entered.

Vivian.

She seemed cautious. Tentative. Shy. Like she was visiting a stranger, unsure of how to start a conversation.

I wanted to speak. I wanted to tell her I loved her. That I didn't mean to hurt her. I wanted her to know that I was lost, confused, and depressed.

But I couldn't say a word. My mouth remained motionless and mute.

My eyes and brain were battling. As much as I wanted to keep my eyes open to try somehow to communicate these thoughts to Vivian, my brain shut them down. I heard some more movement and then silence.

Chapter Twenty-three

Vivian

"Victoria!" Roy bellowed when I walked into the Priceless Pawn. Startled, I suddenly remembered. He thought my name was Victoria from having to show him mom's driver's license last year. I was surprised he remembered.

I almost opened my mouth with the truth but thought, *should I tell him my real name?* It would make it easier if I continued to come in with items to pawn. Keeping up with a fake name could get complicated. But then I thought, *no*, if Mr. McCormick did come looking for his watches and was told Victoria James pawned them, he could hardly go after her.... I mean he did almost kill her. I am sure he wouldn't want to battle Mom for a few thousand dollars. It would be a small price to pay for getting off for attempted murder.

"Hey, I have a couple of amazing watches that I inherited," I said, pulling out the watches and Roy looked at me cautiously.

"Wow, where did you get these?"

"My grandfather," I lied. A harmless lie for Harmony House.

"Hmmm, this one is the Rolex Submariner Date. It retails around $35,000," Roy was looking closely at it. I about peed my pants with excitement. I couldn't believe it. "This one is the Rolex Deepsea. It retails for about $13,000. And these are in mint condition. I rarely get people coming in here willing to pay this kind of cash for a watch. These customers go to a jewelry store or shop online. I can post them for you on eBay and see what we get. I'll take a 25% cut from the sale. Or you can post them yourself."

I thought for a few minutes. My idea that McCormick wouldn't come looking for them any time soon drove me to my decision.

"Ok, you can post them," I said. Then hesitated when looking at the one he called Deepsea. It was magnificent. I liked it better than the more expensive one. Deepsea. I loved the deep sea. Should I keep it? The Submariner was worth way more than I ever expected. Both watches were way more than I ever could have dreamed. If I got $30,000 for the Submariner, wouldn't that really help Harmony House? What would it hurt to keep one?

I glanced at my wrist. I still wore the $40 watch I bought from Roy last summer. I wore it as a reminder. A reminder that anything is possible if you try hard enough. If you want it bad enough. If you are willing to do anything to get it. I looked at the Deepsea. I found myself drawn to it in a way I couldn't explain. I would never wear it. But now I wanted to keep it.

The deep sea was calling my name, pulling me out to its treacherous, royal blue waters.

"You know, let's try selling just this one," I pointed to the Submariner. I knew I would eventually sell the Deepsea, too, but I decided to hold onto it for now. I don't know why, but I suddenly needed to have it. As a reminder. A reminder that Conrad McCormick was going to continue to pay for what he did to mom. And Brianna and Bella and probably countless other girls who were less lucky.

He had me fill out a form which included my phone number and driver's license. I never took Mom's old one out of the zippered compartment of my backpack, so I pulled it out, filling in her license number. We agreed on a minimum bid, and Roy said he would call me when it sold.

Now, I just had to wait.

And find a good hiding place for the Deepsea.

Chapter Twenty-four

Vivian

Mom's state had not changed, and Dad spent his days by her side, hoping for a miracle.

I hadn't seen Leo and knew I needed to talk to him. Dad found the box with the ring in it on the driveway the day after we broke up and put it on my dresser.

With the velvet box in my pocket, I walked down the street to see if Leo was home.

Sheepishly, I stood on his front steps and knocked.

Within a few seconds, he opened the door and cracked his effortless smile. All the worry I had on the way over about how he was going to hate me and be mad at me and maybe even slam the door in my face, evaporated into the muggy, dusky summer air, like warm wet mist.

I was holding the small box and fidgeting with it. He noticed and reached for my hand, "Let's talk." He pulled me around to the backyard where the twinkle lights began to brighten the twilight sky. We stood facing each other and he took the box from me and slid it back into his pocket. Taking both of my hands, he pulled them to his lips and kissed them.

"I love you. I love how smart, confident, and talented you are. I also love how complicated you are, how deeply you think, and how you wrestle with your emotions, trying to make sense of your circumstances, of yourself. I love that you have me guessing about what you might say or do because you aren't afraid to grab what you want and go for something most people wouldn't have the guts to do.

And, I know you hate it when I say this, but you are also incredibly beautiful and sometimes darkly mysterious. You electrify me. And yes, I have had a normal upbringing if that is what you call it, but I love your messy story. You fascinate me. I don't need to rescue you because you rescue yourself, but I would if you needed me. And I am damn sure that if I needed rescuing, you would save me in a minute.

Maybe giving you a ring so soon was a mistake. You are only going to be a sophomore, and I put too much pressure on you. I will keep the ring for the right time,

174

but I still want to be your boyfriend. I don't agree with you stealing those dresses, but I am going to help you work through that pain. If you let me."

I didn't know what to say. We made a promise never to lie to each other. How would he react if he knew I stole the watches from Conrad McCormick? He would hate it. I couldn't do that to him. But I didn't want him out of my life, either. I loved him.

"If it is OK with you, I would like to be friends for now. There is a lot going on with me that I have to sort out. Be patient....... please. I love you. I do. And I can't imagine my life without you in it. You think you like messy and complicated now, but I'm not so sure you always will. Let me get a little less messy. OK?"

His eyes looked hurt, and I had to look down. He pulled me close again, and we stood holding each other, my body melting into his.

I managed to pull away and Leo walked me home. All the way I kept thinking, I hope I can get less messy. I hope this urge to take from Mr. McCormick goes away forever. I hope I can be more like someone Leo deserved. But I wasn't so sure I could do that.

He kissed me gently then brushed his lips on my ear and whispered, "I love you."

I softly uttered, "I love you, too," then slowly turned and walked into my house. I slipped quietly to my

175

room, shut the door, and pulled out a wooden jewelry box from my secret hiding place in the back corner of my closet under a stack of books. I opened the hidden bottom compartment and stared at the Deepsea watch.

I thought, *why did I keep this?* If my reason for stealing was to right a wrong and give to charity, then what did it mean that I wanted to keep this? I told myself that it was a reminder to never forget what that scumbag did, but I didn't need a $13,000 watch to do that. Thirteen thousand dollars would feed a lot of people, clothe a lot of people, give hope to a lot of people. Leo can't date a thief. And keeping this watch made me a flat-out thief – not some heroic Roach Girl Robin Hood that I had been secretly telling myself I was.

I had to sell this watch and give the money to charity. I had to. One day. I promise I will one day.

Just not yet.

Victoria

I woke from resting and saw Collier sitting in the chair in the corner, staring out the window.

What are you thinking? I wanted to ask.

As if reading my mind, he turned to me and said, "I can't provide you with the lavish lifestyle you crave. *I* don't want that kind of life again. I learned that about myself going through rehab. I love the simple life. I bought a small home in a modest neighborhood and I'm teaching and remodeling homes, and I love it. I am very happy....and I'm sober. If you think you can live like that, I want you back. But I mean it, Tory. No designer gowns. No expensive shoes and handbags. No exotic trips. I don't want any of that. But I do want you. If you can live simply. I love you so much, Victoria. I have always loved you."

I felt the tears run down and hit the pillow. I had messed things up so badly, and he still wanted me back. I couldn't believe it. I wanted him back, too. I was done with money. Done. I managed enough strength for a small nod.

That was the answer he needed, and he jumped out of his chair and climbed beside me on the bed, putting one arm over my head on the pillow so as to not hurt me and the other gently over my stomach. He nestled his head into the crevice of my neck, and I felt his tears wet my skin.

Afterward

At a recent charity event for Harmony House, an anonymous donor gave $33,300 in cash. The money had been in a blank envelope placed in the Harmony House collection plate. Sharon couldn't believe it. She said it was the largest single donation to the charity and would help save young girls from the sex trafficking trade. She said she tried to find out who the donor was to thank them, but no one seemed to know.

About the Author

G. Keller is a middle school English teacher. She is married and has two children, two cats, and one dog. When she is not grading papers or hanging out with her family, she enjoys watching The Great British Bake-Off, binge watching a great series, taking long walks thinking up new stories, and writing, of course.

About the Artist

Janelle Bell-Martin is a freelance illustrator working on book illustration, collectible designs, animation final line art and painting.

Roach Girl Three

Money is a monster. Money rules the world. Money stole Vivian's mother. But Vivian has a mission. A mission, a passion, and an obsession. McCormick thinks he rules the world with his money, but Vivian has other plans for him. Why does it bring her such satisfaction to steal from the rich and give to the poor? Why can't she stop? Why did Wyatt Wilson come to Lorenzo Williams High? Wyatt, the rich son of Florida's ex-governor, who represents everything Vivian hates – wealth, power, greed. She wants to hate Wyatt—but she is drawn to him for reasons Leo would never understand. Leo. The love of her life. Good, honest Leo. Leo can't understand her need to steal, nor should he. And he can't understand her growing attraction to Wyatt. Caught in a love triangle, Vivian finds herself drawn to two very different boys, but that is not her biggest problem. McCormick is her biggest problem, and until she gets him out of her life, she will never be able to be with anyone.